DO[...]
YOUR TONGUE?

"Jeffy?" Eagerly I pushed through the doorway. "Hey, Jeffy—"

I froze in disbelief. There were dogmen, a lot of them, all looking at me. They held stunguns. The antiseptic reek grew stronger, and I realized they were using it to mask their scent.

They can't be here, I thought, impossibly, *they can't be in the heart of cat territory, in Hatter's palace—*

I whirled. Scar-face, still grinning, slammed the door. Distantly, I heard it lock.

Dropping to all fours, shapeshifting, I faced the dogs as panther. I snarled, tail lashing.

They just laughed. There were too many of them, at least a dozen, all modded big and powerful.

"Nice pussycat," said the dog nearest me, a total Doberman. He flicked his stungun's switch and it hummed to life.

REMEMORY

JOHN BETANCOURT

POPULAR LIBRARY

An Imprint of Warner Books, Inc.

A Time Warner Company

Excerpts from this novel appeared in *Starshore*, vol. 1, no. 2 (Fall, 1990), in slightly different form, as "Blooding Jeffy."

POPULAR LIBRARY EDITION

Popular Library®, the fanciful P design, and Questar® are registered trademarks of Warner Books, Inc.

Cover illustration by Paul Youll
Cover design by Don Puckey

Popular Library books are published by
Warner Books, Inc.
666 Fifth Avenue
New York, N.Y. 10103

 A Time Warner Company

Printed in the United States of America

First Printing: October, 1990

10 9 8 7 6 5 4 3 2 1

ACKNOWLEDGMENTS

I wish to thank my editor Brian Thomsen and my friends Diane Weinman and Henry Lazarus for critiquing *Rememory* in draft and providing useful comments and insights toward the final version. If you like it, they're responsible; if not, then the blame is mine, since this world and these characters are ultimately my own vision.

1

The guard, a dog, trotted down toward the end of the dock, looking over his shoulder every few steps. He wasn't worried, I thought, just cautious. The briny smell of the ocean hid our scent, and he couldn't possibly have seen us in the dark, in the jumble of packing crates by the warehouse door.

As dogs went, this one was a real bruiser, with the head of a Doberman and the body of a wolf or a husky. He'd have all the latest mods, of course—smugglers always did—and I didn't relish tangling with him. That's why I'd brought Jeffy and Hangman. They'd already taken out the two sentries, and that just left the boss-dog himself.

I felt more than saw Jeffy when he shifted uncomfortably beside me. Glancing over, I noticed his slitted green eyes catching the light.

"*Sst!*" I hissed. "Goggles!"

"Sorry, Slash," he whispered. He pulled them up, and his eyes disappeared in the gloom.

Stupid, stupid, stupid. I let a rumbling growl escape. He knew it didn't matter if the goggles halved our nightsight. That dog was out in the open, plainly lit by spillover from the street lamps a block away. Night or not, he couldn't be missed.

A boat's whistle sounded from out in the bay. I pricked my ears forward and caught the shush of a hull cutting through chop. No engine; they were coasting in. The whistle came again, and this time the dog sat, pulled back his head, and barked coyotelike—two short yips and a low howl, a signal all was well. I smiled to myself. *If only he knew.*

At last the smugglers' boat loomed out of the darkness. I couldn't see it very well, since it had one of those radar-absorbing black plastic hulls and no running lights, but I could pick out silhouettes on deck. Three, I counted, all human.

Steel claws eased from my fingertips. Beside me, Jeffy's breathing turned ragged; he wanted the fight, could almost taste it. Hangman, lost in the dark behind us, merely watched and waited with the patience of a born killer.

One of the men tossed out a mooring line. The dog caught it and stood, suddenly manlike, his bones telescoping out to straighten arms and legs. Quickly he tied the boat to one of the dock's pilings.

The man who'd tossed him the mooring line roughhandled a gangplank into position, as though more concerned with speed than quiet. The other two carried a pair of canisters onto the dock, set them down by the dogman, and said something I couldn't hear. When the dog nodded, they turned and boarded their boat again. Simple and fast, the drop had taken perhaps twenty seconds.

When the dog cast them off, the boat roared out into the bay. It quickly vanished.

The dogman woofed once, then turned and picked up the first canister. His small aircar sat twenty meters away, at the head of the dock. He lugged the canister over, loaded it into the rear storage compartment, then started back for the second one.

"Now," I said to Hangman and Jeffy. "Take him down."

They pulled off their goggles and padded forward, nails clicking on the pavement. In a second they hit the light, Hangman the lean and hungry tiger, Jeffy the sleek black panther, both with spiked collars, both with steel fangs and claws. Both killers.

I waited half a second, then started to the left, following the warehouse wall. I'd take care of the dog's aircar.

As I circled through the stacked crates, I watched the dog-man. He whirled in surprise when he heard Jeffy and Hangman. Barking for help, he shapeshifted, bones contracting, muscles rippling. In seconds he stood half-Doberman, half-husky again. Baring his fangs, he set his feet in case they rushed him. He kept glancing toward the warehouses for help. When his friends didn't come, he snarled in frustration.

Jeffy drifted to the right and Hangman to the left, deathly silent. The dog tried to watch them both, couldn't. He began to back up, pushing the canister with his leg.

Hangman hissed and feinted in. The dog whirled on him, snapping.

And Jeffy sprang at the dog's exposed back. He landed right on target, front claws digging hold, hind claws gouging. The dog yowled in pain and tried to buck him off, but Jeffy held tight.

Then the dog dropped and rolled, and they scrambled across the dock, biting and scratching. Jeffy seized a throat-hold, but lost it when the dog flipped backward and threw him off.

Dripping blood from a dozen wounds, the two growled and tried to stare each other down. Jeffy drew back his lips and snarled mockingly.

The dog rushed him. They clashed again, all claws and teeth, spraying blood and fur.

Then the aircar stood between us and I couldn't see the fight anymore. But I heard it, the dog mostly, still snapping and barking for his friends. Jeffy yowled in sudden pain. No matter, I thought; Hangman had never lost a fight. He'd take care of the dog if Jeffy needed help.

I pulled open the aircar's door. Of course the dog had left it unlocked; no need to fear with two lookouts posted, so far from the heart of the Sprawl. Chuckling, I climbed inside. The ignition cube lay on the seat, and when I pushed it into place, the engine thrummed to life, repeller fields rippling with power. If the impossible happened and the dog killed both Hangman and Jeffy, I'd take off with the first canister already loaded. One of the advantages of braining the operation: a no-lose scenario.

But the impossible didn't happen. The fight was over when I looked up.

I watched as Jeffy, bloody but happy, reverted to human shape. Blood—mostly the dog's, I thought—covered his face. He staggered a bit, but caught himself. Straightening, he walked stiffly to the second canister, picked it up, and carried it proudly toward the aircar. He'd done well: a good first kill.

Hangman, meantime, was dragging the dog's body to the end of the dock. He rolled the corpse into the water, then crouched, tail lashing, to watch it float away. I'd seen him do that before, but never asked why; it seemed personal, some bizarre ritual. You learned not to ask too many questions in our line of work.

I turned back to the aircar's controls and forgot about him; more important things to do now anyway. Quickly I ran the aircar's computer's diagnostics, then plugged in my pocket comp and ran a few of my own. I found the usual two tracking devices, one blatant and one subtle, both of which I yanked and tossed onto the dock. I ran a second check and everything came up clean; the dogs' bosses couldn't hear or follow, so we could use their aircar safely.

Jeffy finished stowing the canister away. Closing the storage compartment, he pulled the rear door open and climbed in behind me.

"Got it, Slash!" he said. "Good job, huh?"

"Excellent," I purred. "You and Hangman make a good team."

Switching on the light, I turned and saw what the dog had done to him. His left ear hung in shreds and two bloody cuts crossed his left eye, swelling it shut. More blood clotted in his sleek black coat from other, less obvious wounds. I winced inwardly; we'd have to get him fixed up. No telling how much internal damage he'd suffered. That dog had been tough all right, a cee-pure bruiser.

"Here." He passed me the dog's tags. "I really got him, huh, Slash? Hangman said the kill's cleanly mine, no doubt about it!"

"Congrats." I jingled the tags for a second, then tucked them into the pouch at my waist. Another trophy for the wall, Jeffy's first kill. "You did great," I said. "Now take a nap. It's a long trip back, and with you bitten up that way, you're going to need your rest."

"Whatever you say, Slash." Instantly he curled up in the back seat and closed his eyes. A little mewing sound escaped him, then he shivered uncontrollably. His adrenaline high had begun to wear off. Soon, I knew, he'd be feeling the pain like little knives all cutting at once.

I dug a sleep capsule from my tool kit and broke it under his nose. A small enough mercy, considering all he'd done for me tonight. He never noticed it, never felt a thing; his mews merely deepened to snores.

Stroking his forehead, I sighed. Poor kit, too young to be dragged into my life of crime. But he'd wanted it, begged to come along. And I didn't have the strength to deny him —as I had denied him nothing throughout his childhood.

I caught a whiff of the lilac-scented sleepgas and, for an

instant, my head swam drunkenly. I opened the window and took several deep breaths to clear my thoughts.

Hangman had finished his death ritual. Standing, he strutted back to the aircar, still in tigerform, and leaped in beside me. Blood flecked his coat; he began licking himself clean.

"You okay?" I said.

He nodded. Never much of a talker, our Hangman.

I energized the repeller fields, and slowly the aircar lifted. We skipped up and over the abandoned warehouses, a block inland. Here street lamps gave plenty of light, showing the burnt-out wrecks of groundcars and aircars, the heaps of trash and refuse, the empty shells of buildings—we truly *had* come to the cesspool of the Americas. It would be weeks if not months before the dogs' bodies were found and reported, if they ever were.

A hundred meters down, I pulled into a small, dark alley. We'd stashed our own aircar here the night before.

Hangman was up and out even before I pulled the ignition cube. While he saw to the canisters, I busied myself with Jeffy. My adopted kit was all skin and bones, but he still weighed more than I'd thought he would; something about the increased density of enhanced muscles . . .

I levered him up and draped him over my shoulders in a fireman's carry, staggering a bit under the burden. Soft, rotting things squished underfoot as I carried him to our aircar, the overpowering stench of mold and decay rising around me.

Finally, though, I got him in the back seat. There he curled up again, looking happy and comfortable from the sleepgas. He wouldn't be hurting for a while yet. His nose felt hot, though—not a good sign. How much damage had the dog done?

Panting, I leaned back in the seat to catch my breath. Plans were my specialty, not physical labor; I was in lousy shape and knew it. That's why I needed Jeffy and Hangman to do my muscle. That, and my desire to live to a ripe old age.

"Slash, come out and see this," Hangman said, in an oddly strangled voice. *"Now."*

That was one of the longest speeches I'd ever heard him give, and his tone sent chills down my back. *Something's wrong*, I thought. I pulled myself up and hurried around to the stolen aircar.

He had the storage compartment open and the lids off the canisters—he hadn't been able to wait to see our haul. I pressed up beside him. Drugs, this time? Stolen electronics? We'd scored them all over the years. I knew the market and would get top 'dollar, no matter what.

As I leaned forward, the sour-sweet smell of decaying flesh hit me first. My nose wrinkled; my whiskers twitched. I strained to see in the darkness and almost threw up when I realized what they held.

Inside each canister, carefully packed in bubble plastic, lay a severed human head.

2

"I don't like this," Hangman said.

Stunned, I didn't reply. I just stood there, not knowing what to think. Why would they smuggle heads? My hands felt weak and my stomach knotted mercilessly. When I swallowed, I found a lump in my throat.

Finally I set the lids back onto the canisters and tamped them down, hard. I didn't like the look of this. What had we blundered into? The dogs wouldn't save body parts from routine murders; far too risky. And they certainly wouldn't smuggle heads into the country without reason. No, I'd missed something important, something less than obvious. *In any case, they've got to be valuable*, a voice inside me said. *Find out who wants them and half the problem's gone*.

But something else, something deeper and perhaps wiser, whispered, *Get out while you still can. Dump them in the river*.

"Slash?" Hangman said.

I swallowed my fears. It wouldn't do to let Hangman see my unease. What could it hurt to keep them around, at least for a while? They posed a puzzle for me, and I hated unsolved puzzles.

Softly, I said: "This isn't the place." I moved to take the first canister, but Hangman leaned an elbow on it.

"So what do you want me to do?" I demanded. "I didn't know they were running body parts."

He didn't answer.

I said, "Since they went to so much trouble, they've got to be valuable, right? All we have to do is find out how."

He thought about that. For a second I'd thought we were going to have an argument (what share would he and Jeffy get for stealing heads, anyway?), but then he shrugged.

"Later, then," he said. Picking up the canister, he carried it over to our aircar and put it into the back with Jeffy.

Later suited me. An alley ten blocks from our strike didn't feel exactly safe, especially not with what we'd found. Drugs I could deal with, or hot hardware, but heads would need some research, some extra think-time. Picking up the second canister, I carried it to our aircar and stored it away too. There would be time enough to find out what we had when we were safely away.

Why would they smuggle heads?

Hangman slid into the driver's seat and brought the engine to roaring life. I strapped in beside him, still musing.

The only person I knew who might come up with answers was half-crazed, but in a different way from Hangman and Jeffy and me. *Esteban Grammatica.* The bodyman who'd made me cat. If anyone could make sense of the heads, he could.

I told Hangman, and ten seconds later, we were headed north, toward the smog-shrouded Sprawl of Washington-Baltimore-Philadelphia. The endless gray streets, the factories churning out smoke and chemical fogs, the miles-long stretches of featureless brick row houses: home territory for our little band. Here and there little pockets of buildings gleamed brighter than the rest, marking turbostations or business districts or party zones for the glitterfolk and their friends.

An hour later we hit centerSprawl, and here things were liveliest of all. Neon-outlined skyscrapers towered over the streets, their upper floors shrouded in haze, their lower floors drowning in people. Spotlights on their roofs probed smogbanks with fingers of light, darting first one way, then another. Twice their beams transfixed us before sweeping on.

Even this far up I could see the huge crowds massing in the streets, the glitterfolk in their glowing, extravagant costumes, the punks with dazzle-spiked hair, the hackers and skinheads and all the other streeters in full regalia. Nothing ever changed in the Sprawl. It seethed with life.

We circled down between buildings, into a crowded alley. Hangman left no doubt about his intentions; he flashed on our aircar's landing lights and cut repeller fields to half power.

We dropped fast enough to make me gulp, and the people below scattered in record time rather than be crushed. When we grounded with a *thump*, Hangman powered down.

I checked Jeffy and found him still asleep. His lips had pulled back a bit in a half-grimace; pain had set in. We'd soon have him right, I thought. When I touched his shoulder, he opened his one good eye and squinted blearily at me.

"Where—?" he mumbled. Groaning, he sat up and rubbed his head.

"The bodyshop. Almost there. Come on."

When Hangman popped the aircar's doors, unfiltered air rushed in. I gagged and wheezed; I'd never gotten used to the centerSprawl mix, thick and foul as open sewage, carbon dioxide, and countless noxious chemicals from the factories could make it.

I pawed nose filters from my pocket and shoved them into place. They were uncomfortable, but they masked the worst of the stink, made it at least tolerable. My eyes began to burn; I blinked quickly, fighting back tears. We'd be indoors soon enough, fortunately for me.

Jeffy eased out of the aircar and stood unsteadily on the pavement, breathing deeply, seeming to enjoy the city air. He'd been born here, I remembered, among the streeters, before finding his way to catkind. Going cat had probably saved his life. Most of his friends had long ago died in knife fights or streeter brawls, or tranqued their minds to jelly with custom drugs in the skyeye bars, he'd once told me. I believed him. Only a few—a fortunate few—escaped the streets these days, and they usually ended up among the ranks of the dayworkers—a dead end in itself, in a different sort of way. One of the problems in a society as rigidly stratified as ours had become: it took someone exceptional, someone with the drive to succeed, to escape. Or someone extremely lucky. Jeffy had been lucky.

The crowds surged around us, bands of glitterdressed men and women from the burbs mostly, here on St. Jude Street, where all the quaint and costly little boutiques could be found. A few beggars here and there, a few hucksters with blankets of jewelry or incense spread on the pavement before them, a few animen (not like us, but birds strutting their feathers), and even a few I couldn't quite recognize, but just as strange and outlandish as the rest.

"Slash—"

Jeffy's knees gave and I caught him, made him lean on my shoulder. We started forward, slowly working our way toward the bodyshop. I glanced back and saw Hangman pulling out the two canisters. Balancing them, he closed up the aircar and activated its security system, then jogged to catch up.

Half a block ahead, a neon sign jutted over the street. It said ANIMEN-R-Us in bright pink letters that danced back and forth on little feet. If you needed fixing, Esteban Grammatica could do it faster and better than anybody else. Other bodyshops underpriced him, but could never compete with his extra services—like secrecy, guaranteed. He kept his bribes paid up, so the feet left him strictly alone.

As we neared ANIMEN-R-Us, a pair of dogmen exited, barking and nipping at each other. Recent converts, I thought, feeling old and jaded. They'd gone for the flashy look, golden retrievers both, with long whiskers and beautifully groomed pelts. Still barking, they pranced up the street and vanished amidst the glitterfolk.

I helped Jeffy up the steps and pushed the door open. Somewhere in the back, a bell jangled.

We entered a small, dim room full of bubbling chemtanks. Little had changed in the bodyshop since my last visit. Tiny vidscreens on the walls still showed *New! Exciting!* animal mods, holos still pictured the best and the brightest of Grammatica's creations, and inside the tanks still floated enhanced human and animal body parts. Little signs marked them: "Hedgehog" and "Rat" were on sale this week, I noted.

I pulled my nose filters and put them away. The air was a bit musky inside, but clean enough, certainly breathable.

Settling Jeffy on one of the benches, I moved to the vids. They flashed onto my form and brought up the latest cat mods. Several new brands of cat-eyes interested me; I palmed the screen and watched performance parameters flow past. Impressive, I thought. Somehow the Koreans had weaseled around the human optic-nerve limitations and come up with a truer nightsight. I wanted them, had to have them.

The shimmerscreen separating the display room from the operating theaters suddenly crackled with sparks as fat old Esteban Grammatica himself pushed through. Grammatica had always been the quintessential animan. He'd done up his body in snakeskin, and the scales shimmered with iridescent patterns, cool and leathery. His forked tongue flickered briefly across thin lips; his small black eyes studied me. Then, dispassionately, his gaze swept over to the bench, to Jeffy.

"Well, Slash," he said, very smooth, very slick, "I see your kit's gone fighting again, yes?"

It was a running joke by now. He knew what we did; I paid him well enough for his confidentiality. I just nodded and said, "Can you fix him up?"

"Have I ever failed you?"

"Course not," I said. "You're the best."

Laughing, he slithered closer, bending to see Jeffy's damaged face, noting the wounds on chest and legs. He dismissed them with a wave.

"A little skin, a new eye, a few nips and tucks inside. No problem. Two hours, yes. I'm out of black panther, though; have to make do with leopard skintights. Or I can send out?"

"Leopard's fine. Can the dog do it?"

"Why?"

"Got something to show you." I pointed to the canisters Hangman had set by Jeffy. "Private-room stuff."

"Paul!" he bellowed. His smile turned oily, professional. "Fun time! Got a cat-job for you."

Paul trotted out through the shimmerscreen. He was one of Grammatica's specials, with a German shepherd's body and a human's hands and face. He grinned, tail wagging, when he saw us. Dog or not, it was hard to dislike Paul. He'd done maintenance on me more times than I could count, and he'd never made a mistake. Genetically programmed not to, Grammatica had once said, not that I believed it.

"You too, Slasher?" Paul asked, too eager. "Or just Jeffy?"

"Just Jeffy this time," I said with a laugh. "You'll get your paws on me soon enough, I bet. Saw some new eyes I want."

"I already ordered the Korean eyes on the promo tape for

you," Grammatica said. "They should get here next week, straight from the lab."

"Great!" I said in delight.

"And I ordered a set for Hangman and Jeffy. Expensive, but worth it for the best."

At that, I just nodded. Expensive indeed, but I knew I'd pay; I always did. I took upgrades at every chance; that was one of the reason's I'd lived so long in my profession.

Grammatica and Paul took Jeffy's arms and half carried, half dragged him through the shimmerscreen, into a spotless white corridor. Hangman handed me one of the canisters, and we followed. All the while Grammatica explained to Paul what he wanted done, in graphic detail.

The back rooms had the sharp, sterile smell of a hospital, but I scarcely noticed; I'd begun thinking about those two heads again, about all the questions they raised. Why save them? Why smuggle them into the United States? How were dogs involved?

We passed rooms full of operating tables, odd chrome-and-steel machines, multibladed electric bone-saws, and other devices whose functions I couldn't begin to guess— and didn't particularly want to know. Grammatica could do almost anything with animalform and humanoform sculpting, given enough time and enough money; his was the most complete bodyshop I'd ever seen in private hands, and his work matched anything the big corporations could do. Plus he put a little something extra into his work, like a true artist rather than a mere mechanic.

He and Paul put Jeffy into one of the smaller rooms. As we watched, they gassed him unconscious. Then Paul took off Jeffy's spiked collar and untabbed Jeffy's fur skintights at the throat, peeling them away, revealing web-scarred pink skin and rows of dark nipples, all blotched now with huge blue-black bruises. What I'd taken for major wounds seemed little more than scratches under the bright operating lamps. Lucky thing Jeffy's fur had slacked the damage.

Once Paul had his instructions, Grammatica ushered us out. An electric scalpel's whir carried through the closed door.

"Now," the snakeman said, "you have something to show me, yes? Will my office do?"

"I'd suggest someplace easily cleaned," I said.

His eyebrows arched in interest, and he led us into the next operating theater, shoving aside wheeled instrument trays. Drawing a plastic sheet from a storage cabinet, he spread it over a stainless-steel table.

I set my canister down and unsealed the lid. The stench of rotting flesh seemed to come at me in waves; I held my breath. Upending the first canister, I gentled the head out for Grammatica to examine, then moved back a safe distance.

He scarcely blinked. In the bright light, the head looked distinctly unreal, the flesh gray-green, the eyes bulging, the lips swollen and purple.

"I doubt I could culture it," Grammatica said slowly. "He's been dead far too long for that. I might get a viable DNA sample and work a clone up from that, yes, but the expense—"

"I don't want a clone," I said. "I want to know what makes these heads—there's one in the other canister, too—worth smuggling into the country." Quickly I outlined what had happened, how we'd gotten them. I had no secrets from Esteban Grammatica; in fact, I gave him a cut of every job for his help, which covered not only routine bodyshop repairs like Jeffy's, but information like we needed now.

"Ah," he said when I finished. He pulled plastic gloves from a drawer. His arms and fingers were curiously supple, more like miniature snakes than anything else, and it was interesting to watch him worm the gloves on. When he finished, he picked up the head and held it close to his face, studying it. His eyeballs rolled back in their sockets, revealing a second set of pupils, these smaller and steel-gray, for microscopic detail work, I knew.

"The skin's artificial," he said after a moment's hesitation. "Cheap Mexican stuff. The man had a rush ident change, I would guess. Eyes . . . real, but new corneas. Hair's clearly synthetic. Ah? What's this . . . *here*?"

He found a catch I never could have seen and flicked it. The hair peeled back, revealing a metal plate set into the skull. He probed, but could find no way of getting it open. "Odd . . . ," he murmured. He selected a small needlelike tool from one of the tables and worked on in silence, sweat beading his forehead, forked tongue darting across his lips every few seconds. I leaned closer to see.

At last he set the head down. "Well done," he said. "It seems they actually got the bone to grow into the metal. I've never seen the like before. Exquisite job, better than I could do, though I hate to admit it."

"But what's it *for*?" I demanded.

"Tomorrow," he said. "Come back early. I will get the skin and the flesh off in my culture tanks tonight. Easy enough, yes."

"Do you think it's anything valuable?" I asked.

"Valuable? I would give a fortune to know how they did that skull-plate surgery alone. As for what it does?" He shrugged. "Tomorrow."

Carefully he set the head back into its canister, then shooed us into the hall to wait for Jeffy.

3

Jeffy's repairs didn't take all that long. When he strutted out in his leopard skintights two hours later, looking good, truly good, and knowing it, I gave him the once-over. His new eye and ear matched the old ones perfectly, of course; or perhaps both had been replaced. Regardless, it was the results that mattered, and I couldn't tell he'd been injured at all. Esteban Grammatica had worked his usual wonders.

"Great job, huh?" Jeffy said, dropping to all fours and shapeshifting. As leopard, he bounded forward to rub against my hip, then drew back and mock-growled.

I laughed easily. "About time," I said, standing. "Lots to do tomorrow. Let's get going."

Hangman and I had been watching a documentary on a colony of penguinmen in Alaska. It had been the only entertainment vid we could find in the outer room. If we'd stayed much longer, boredom would have driven me crazy.

"Don't forget," Grammatica told me. "Tomorrow."

I showed him my fangs, an almost-smile. "I won't forget."

* * *

We headed north. The sky had already begun to pale in the east, a gray smudge that would soon turn pink from the rising sun. I leaned back and tried to doze, closing my eyes and letting Hangman fly, but sleep eluded me. My thoughts kept turning to the severed heads, to the mystery inside them. Some new mods, clearly—but what? And how were dogs and their masters involved?

When next I looked up, the sun had risen. Row houses were flowing like an endless brick ocean beneath us. To our right and left, the air seethed with aircars, huge lumbering transit platforms, and all manner of other aircraft: all the drones heading off to work, I thought. I hated mornings in the Sprawl most of all, hated the complacent masses, their antlike behavior, their endless conformity. Once I'd been like them. But those memories were too painful, too raw in my mind, and I forced them away.

A cheerful thought: we were nearing cat territory, a place once called Fishtown, when it had been in oldcity Philadelphia. Here, the row houses seemed more random, forming a maze of dark paths and alleyways. Streets had long been blocked to anything but pedestrian traffic, and as the buildings rose higher and higher, the ground had grown more shadowy. To us, with our quiet, calm ways and nightsight eyes, it seemed heaven. So catkind adopted Fishtown as its home.

Nobody knew how many catmen lived here. I'd once heard an estimate of twenty thousand, but surely that seemed too high—though I had to admit, when prowling and playing the alleys by night, I recognized few other cats.

Entering Fishtown airspace, Hangman circled us down. My home nestled in one of the central blocks, five stories tall like most of the other row houses, not visibly in good repair, in no way different or interesting to the casual observer. Of course, that was deliberate illusion: I'd put millions of newdollars into not only interior restorations, but security measures. If you screwed with dogs and smugglers, you had to watch your back, I'd long ago found out.

Hangman keyed our passcode into the computer-link, and the roof defenses let us land atop my row house. This time I didn't bother with nose filters; no need, this far north. I could tolerate the air here.

Hangman popped the doors. As we climbed out, I turned slowly, taking a careful survey of adjoining rooftops. Lots of antennae and microwave dishes, a good number of sleek black aircars, a small flock of gray pigeons—nothing new or unusual or even very interesting. Few cats stirred this early, and I saw no signs of life beyond the traffic overhead.

Good enough. I crossed to a pair of durasteel doors and palmed their handpad. The house computer chirped a welcome as it recognized me.

A second later, the doors opened, revealing a large lift. Warning lights across the back wall showed green: all clear. None of the house monitors had caught anyone or anything probing our defenses.

"Safe," I told Hangman and Jeffy. I followed them in, then the doors closed and the lift started down.

"Will you go with me to the wall tonight?" Jeffy asked.

"Of course," I said. "I wouldn't miss it."

Hangman merely grunted.

When night fell, Jeffy came to get me. He wore the dogtags around his neck, and they jingled as he moved. I'd been ready for some time, of course, but couldn't let him know that: this was his night, and I had to let his excitement build.

"Coming, coming!" I called. I strolled from my bedroom as though we had all the time in the world.

Together we shapeshifted and, side by side, padded down the hallway to the stairs. The paintings on the walls, the carpet underfoot, it all felt comfortable, even in catform. Too long away, I thought.

Reaching ground level, I sat, tail curled around my feet. Jeffy looked over his shoulder, noticed I'd stopped, and came back.

"Slash?" he asked. "Everything okay?"

"Let's hear your story," I said patiently.

"Huh?"

"When you stand on the wall, you have to brag your kill. You can't very well say we ambushed smugglers. That's our secret. You have to have another story, one that's just as convincing."

"I know that," he said, sounding a bit hurt. "I'm not *stupid*, Slash!"

"Still," I said, "we don't want them to know it's not the truth. Practice makes perfect. Let me hear it."

So he sat and, slowly and plainly, told me how the three of us had come across a lone dog guarding a centerSprawl warehouse. He'd been big, modified total Doberman from nose to tail, and he'd made fun of us. Hangman had wanted to take him down, but Jeffy'd asked to do it instead.

It had been a bloody fight (and he described it in detail, borrowing most of the action from his fight with the dog on the dock), but he'd won fair and square. He'd pulled the dog's tags to prove it. Afterward, we'd taken Jeffy to a bodyshop to celebrate, and that's how he'd gotten fixed up as leopard.

"Excellent," I said, a bit surprised. The story didn't need a bit of touch-up. He'd obviously planned it out ahead of time. *Makes up for his watching the dog without goggles*, I thought.

"I'm glad you like it, Slash," he said. "So let's go, huh?"

"Sure."

Standing, I opened the side door. Together, quiet as two ghosts, we slipped into the long, dark shadows of twilight.

Hangman had been waiting outside. He joined us, matching stride, as we hit the street.

Grinning, he said, "Careful, Slash."

"Why?"

"You'll burst from pride."

I laughed. Pride: I felt it, certainly. My kit had killed a dog single-handed!

Other catmen were out now. As Jeffy jingled past, they turned to look.

"We're going for the wall," I told them. "Jeffy killed a dog!"

Several whooped encouragement, and the rest called congratulations. Most dropped what they were doing to join us, and together we followed Jeffy down the street.

It rapidly became a walking party. We laughed and joked and called to all the other cats we saw, and most of them joined us too. As word spread, catmen flooded in from all directions, slipping down from their houses, sliding in from the shadows.

First dozens, then hundreds strong, we marched through the streets, Jeffy at our head. With every cheer, with every shout, his stride seemed to lengthen. Throwing back his head, he roared. The crowd roared in response, and I joined in. The primal urge to band together, to gather into a pack, this was what it meant to be a catman, I thought.

By the time we had wound through all the streets in Fishtown, over a thousand catmen jammed the street behind us. Only then did Jeffy turn for the wall.

It stood three meters high and ten meters long in a small park in the center of Fishtown. The rusting remains of children's playthings surrounded it: swing sets, jungle gyms, carousels. All the trees had been cut back, so it stood isolated, in plain view: *the wall*, clearly and unmistakably.

As cats filtered in from the trees, surrounding him, Jeffy

strutted forward. The moon was up by then, so bright and full nobody could miss him when he took his place. I could feel all eyes turn his way. This was his moment of glory, his true coming of age.

"Up you go," I whispered. "They're all yours."

Without hesitation, he leaped as high as he could, hooking claws over the top. Digging in, he scrambled up and stood silhouetted against the skyline. There he did a little prancing dance of triumph, first back and forth, then snarling and snapping at an invisible opponent. Throwing back his head, he roared, a savage, primal sound.

The cats around me shifted, eyes gleaming, tails lashing. A collective moan of anticipation rose from them.

Pausing, balanced, Jeffy screamed to all who could hear: "I met a single dog in fair combat, and beat him! I stole his tags! *I own his soul!*"

He drew the dogtags from around his neck and held them up for all to see. They gleamed like silver in the moonlight. Then Jeffy cast them down. They chinked into the pile of tags that other cats had taken over the years.

A yowling cry of acclamation went up. Jeffy strutted right, then left again. Throwing back his head, he roared, and a hundred, a thousand voices raised as one. We screamed our hatred and our power and our strength. We screamed our *freedom.*

As the sound trailed away, Jeffy leaped down in one swift motion. Proudly he rose against the wall, dug in his steel claws, and scratched his mark across all the older marks. His would stand foremost until the next dog-kill.

Around me, cats began to cheer. I felt a rising pride; this was *my* kit, *my* Jeffy who'd killed a dog in fair combat. I threw back my head and roared too.

Then all the other cats were milling around Jeffy, calling for the story of his adventure, as I'd known they would. And Jeffy began the tale just as he'd told it to me earlier. In the night, in the dark with all the other cats so close, with spirits running so wild, they would have believed anything. And Jeffy's story sounded so convincing that I almost believed it myself.

I sat back on my haunches, ears pricked forward, whiskers twitching, and listened with the best of them. It was Jeffy's night, after all, and he deserved the glory of his kill. Tomorrow my time would come.

4

I left my house early the next morning. I hadn't been able to reach Hangman (he'd always adamantly refused to tell me where he lived; considering our profession, I didn't blame him), and Jeffy's night out celebrating with his friends had left him so hung over he wouldn't have been much use. So I went alone and caught a transit platform to centerSprawl, switched lines at a turbostation, and eventually arrived at Grammatica's shop.

Finding the place locked tight, I buzzed and waited impatiently. Paul finally opened the front door. To my surprise, he wore a tattered apron and held a scrub brush in one hand. Over his shoulder I saw a mop and a bucket of sudsy water by the far wall.

"Boss's in his office," he said, moving back to let me enter. "Expecting you, Slasher."

"Get him to hire someone else to scrub the floors," I said. "He can afford it."

Paul woofed a laugh. "Only trusts me. No outsiders working here, no security leaks."

"It's still a waste."

"Thanks, Slasher. Oh, and the boss has a tech with him —dangerous fellow, lots of odd custom mods. Did the work himself and had Grammatica install it. Subtle."

"Thanks," I said. "I'll bring you a bone next time."

Paul laughed again and moved aside. I entered; he bolted the door behind me.

This was the first time I'd been inside ANIMEN-R-Us before business hours, and with all the lights and holos off, it looked more like a pet store than anything else. If you squinted, the eyes and fingers and bolts of animal skin in the chemtanks became fish, and the foaming, frothing sounds blended into a soothing oceanlike murmur.

Paul went back to scrubbing floor tiles. He whistled cheerfully, seeming to enjoy his work.

I scarcely noticed. I had more important things to worry about—like the tech Grammatica had brought in. *Why?* I wondered uncomfortably, starting down the hall. The walls looked old and gray without the holos covering them. Even the shimmerscreens were gone. *Why would Grammatica need him?* Never trust a tech: it was an adage among animen. They were too self-absorbed, too cold and remote from their humanity. I'd had bad experiences with them before . . . in fact, they'd almost killed me once, when I was young and just starting out in the dog-raiding game. I'd swiped a dog's shipment of datachips—nothing fancy, just gambling records it turned out—and I'd gone straight to the first tech house I saw.

They took one look at the chips' contents and called the dogs. The reward had been worth more to them than the information.

I'd escaped, obviously, but it had been a close thing. And since then I'd always hated techs, hated dealing with them. When I had to, I always used middlemen.

Grammatica's office lay at the rear of the building, in an old-style paneled room. A real wood desk sat before shelves packed with paper record-books and datatapes. I could not help but notice the two skulls sitting in the center of the desk. Both had metal plates showing, so I knew they were the remains of the heads I'd stolen.

". . . and that's why it's not for sale yet," Grammatica was saying to a tall, thin man I'd never seen before.

Both shut up when I walked in. The man's shoulders were squared and his spine stiff, giving the impression of military bearing. But when he turned and looked full-face at me, I knew, somehow, that he'd never served a day in his life— his eyes held a certain fire, his expression a certain crazed intensity, that left no doubt he was used to giving orders, not taking them: a tech like the dog had said, and not just any tech but one of their leaders, if I guessed rightly.

He seemed to measure me up, then dismiss me: *No threat*, I thought. My whiskers twitched. Perhaps it was my pride, but I didn't like that, not at all.

"Am I intruding?" I growled, half hoping.

"No," said Grammatica. He waved me to a chair. "I was just showing Pietr what we had."

"Good." I slouched into my seat, tail lashing, and looked to Pietr. "You're the tech. So?"

"Tech is so sloppy a word."

"Specialist, then." I looked at the skulls. "What are they?"

"Polytacteural encode/decoders," he said. "PEDs for short." He picked up one of the skulls and turned it over and over in his hands. "These are new, probably out of China, right? I received the specs for a similar model several weeks ago. They list as predevelopmental, nowhere near testing stage yet. They certainly should not exist as working implants. Someone is playing games with the reports."

"Poly-whatsits?" I said. "What are they?"

"They are . . ." He hesitated, downjargoning into something I could follow. "Call them memory enhancers, right?

They tag into the central nervous system for power and information relays. If the specs are correct, eyes and ears become recorders for later playback. Instant total recall of anything you see or hear while wearing one."

"They're for spies," I said, shocked.

"They were originally planned as a new form of entertainment: just plug in a data disk and relive any recorded experience. Then the Chinese military became involved in the research—they must have seen the potential wartime applications."

"But the Chinese army didn't kill these two," I said. "Smugglers had them."

"Our best guess," Grammatica said, "is that the two heads belonged to test subjects who went astray. Someone grabbed them for their implants. All the murderers needed were the heads, so that's what they took. Doubtless some U.S. lab would have removed the PEDs for analysis."

It sounded convincing. Everyone knew the toughest of the streeters, the dogs, sometimes worked for underground techs. If the heads were bound for an illicit lab, that was the way they would've been smuggled into this country. Suddenly it all made a horrible amount of sense.

"I want them," Pietr said.

That caught my interest. I said, "Make an offer."

"Five hundred million. A credit transfer—name an account."

That was more than I'd ever gotten for a single job, but the amount made me uneasy. Lots of alarms would go off if that much got dumped into one of my accounts, even the Swiss one I sometimes used to distance myself from especially hot payments. I didn't particularly want the scrutiny. And I didn't particularly want a tech knowing my account numbers. All those bright boys with data implants could move through the electronic banking system whenever they wanted to, doing whatever they felt like. I'd heard enough banking horror stories to make me distrustful. No, a cash transaction seemed much more appealing.

Data retrieval . . . and memory enhancement. I could see a lot of uses for those implants. If a tech were offering five hundred million for the technology hot, it had to be worth a dozen times as much.

"Three hundred million, cash," I said. When he didn't blink, I added on impulse, "For one."

"No!" he said. His lips whitened with rage. "I want both. I cannot risk a competitor having one."

"Three hundred million," I said, "and I will guarantee nobody in competition with you gets the extra one."

He hesitated. "Guarantee with what?"

"My life." I said it seriously, and he took it that way. He studied me for a long minute, and I felt the tension between us, an almost tangible thing. I didn't move, didn't change expression except to half close my slitted cat-eyes. Unreadable, I knew. I had practiced it enough.

Pietr looked at Grammatica. When the snakeman nodded almost imperceptibly, a bit of the tension eased. With Grammatica backing me, Pietr would have no choice but to accept. If he wanted the implants that badly, others would too.

Pietr seemed to realize that. At last he sucked in a deep breath—and offered me his hand.

I shook it solemnly.

"Agreed," he said.

It took several hours to work through the details, with Grammatica arbitrating disagreements, but at last we concluded our deal. My end seemed fair, but not exceptional—especially considering the merchandise—and I could tell the tech felt the same way about his end.

We shook hands once more, then he left. He'd have the cash by that afternoon, he'd promised. Doubtless he needed time to raise it; three hundred million was quite a bit to have lying around as ready cash, even for techs.

Grammatica leaned back at his desk, serpentine hands coiled over his roll of a stomach, and said, "You kept the second PED for yourself, yes?"

I supposed I had, and nodded. "If you think it's safe."

"The Chinese clearly had them working. Since I see no damage to either PED, they should work now."

"But there's a risk," I said.

"Yes . . . and there's a risk in crossing the street. And a risk in breathing the Sprawl airmix. The greatest risk will come from those who lost the devices if they find out you have one."

"I'll take my chances."

"But should you? You're my favorite cat, Slash, and I would not enjoy losing you. Yes?"

That made me pause. The dogs had murdered to get the PEDs, severed two men's heads. I shivered a bit: nasty business all the way around. But—*total recall*. It would prove immensely useful in my line of work. No need to steal papers; just look them over and make copies at my leisure. I could learn bank-account sequences if I saw them even once. And if someone quick-keyed a safe combination, I could dig it out from memory. *Total recall*. Quite a useful trick indeed.

My decision was made. It had been made when I first learned what the PEDs did.

"When can you implant mine?" I asked.

He picked up one of the skulls, almost caressing it. "The operation will be fast but messy. And Pietr won't be back for several hours. . . ."

"You won't have any problem with the installation?"

He tapped a datachip before him. "Pietr brought a copy of the specs. It's a tricky bit of work, yes, but I can certainly do it for you."

"Then," I whispered before I could back out, "now's the time." And I thought of Grammatica's policy: *Secrecy, guaranteed*.

He stood, still holding the skull, and motioned me toward the operating theaters. If he seemed a little reluctant, or a little sad, I put it down to my imagination. What could possibly go wrong? *Nothing*. I was his favorite catman, and he'd make sure I stayed safe.

5

Darkness.

My head throbbed. Groaning, I tried to sit up, but a mountainous weight crushed my chest. I couldn't move, couldn't breathe.

—sitting in a hotel room overlooking an office complex in the background is the Eiffel Tower I have a rifle in my hand I raise it to the window and watch the viewfinder zero in on target—

"Easy," someone said from a great distance. "Are the second-phase relays working yet?"

"No," someone else said. "Misfire."

"Ah . . . try again. The optic nerve, yes?"

I knew those voices, I thought. Grammatica? Paul?

—sitting in a hotel room the Eiffel Tower—

"No, no, silly pup. *Here.*"

—I am sitting—

Darkness again.

When I opened my eyes, the world blurred in shades of gray. *Something's wrong*, I thought. I tried to speak, but my tongue felt numb.

"You are safe," I heard Grammatica saying across a great distan e. "The operation went well."

Cold drops splashed into my eyes. My retinas began to burn, and I gasped in sudden pain. I jerked back and tried to rub my face, but someone seized my hands and forced them down. Tears rolled down my cheeks. I wheezed, breath coming short.

And abruptly the room dropped into focus. The dark shape looming over me became Paul. He leaned forward, licked my nose, and whined a bit. Behind him, at the shiny steel equipment, Esteban Grammatica cleaned away wads of bloodstained gauze and started sterilizing his instruments.

I sat up, and a sharp, blinding pain hit me behind the eyes like nothing I'd ever felt before. I moaned helplessly.

Grammatica merely called, "Breathe deeply. Stop hyperventilating."

Pressing my eyes shut, I willed Grammatica and Paul away, willed myself alone with my misery. Why did it feel like something had gone wrong? Why did I feel like crawling into a hole and dying? Even the worst of the catmods hadn't affected me this badly.

Paul shook my shoulder, and I snapped at him. His fingers danced nimbly away from my fangs, but I got a nip of fur, dank and foul-tasting as only synthetics can be.

"I said, breathe!" Grammatica told me again.

Growling in misery, hating him, hating myself, I did as instructed and sucked in a deep lungful of air. It reeked of disinfectant and sleepgas, but it somehow steadied my innards. If I didn't move a muscle, I thought, I just might live.

"How do you feel now?" the snakeman asked, pushing Paul aside and bending to look at my eyes. His expression had a strange intensity.

"Sick," I hissed. "My head's killing me!"

"Interesting."

"It doesn't fucking well *feel* interesting! Give me something for it!"

"Not a good idea. You must let your senses adjust to the new input devices. Compare it to getting new eyes—soon the headaches fade, yes?"

I pulled another deep breath. Then, slowly, trying to cause myself as little pain as possible, I reached around and probed the back of my head . . . but found no tenderness, and not a bit of swelling. Grammatica had done his usual brilliant job.

I said as much. Then I forced myself to look around, and the room swung crazily, double-imaged walls drifting in and out of focus. I pressed my eyes shut and felt like throwing up.

"Another," Grammatica said.

Taking a second deep, shuddering breath, I managed to calm my stomach. The room focused once more.

I said, "So how do I turn the damned thing on and off?"

"Everything you see and hear is automatically recorded—there is a twenty-minute event buffer. You store events by saying a command sequence. Here." He handed me a small card with BLACK RABBIT neatly hand-printed on it. "I programmed this one."

"Let me see if I understand," I said. "Whenever I say this, the last twenty minutes of my life will be permanently stored?"

"Yes."

"How do I call up specific recordings?"

"Merely think about them. They will appear like normal memories, but in full detail—more like watching a vid than anything else, I would say."

"How much storage space?"

"Around five hundred hours, I would guess. And the PED disk can be removed and replaced with a blank whenever you want. If you ever find a blank one, that is.'' He chuckled. ''But fifteen hundred events should last you decades, if you are careful.''

''I can imagine,'' I said dryly.

They'd skinned off my skintights before the operation; no sense getting them bloodied. I shrugged away the sheet and stood barefoot on the cold tiled floor. A mirror across the room caught my image. I saw a creature one hundred and seventy centimeters tall, with the body of a man and the head of a cat. Eight nipples down my chest and stomach, a pattern of web-scars from all the surgery (why have them removed when they didn't show under the skintights?), faint traces of steel-gray hair across my chest and around my genitals.

My head ached fiercely, of a sudden, and I looked away. *I'm getting too old for this*. Nevertheless, I forced myself to action. My skintights lay draped over a chair; I picked them up and pulled them on.

''Can you bring a 'phone?'' I said. ''I've got to call Jeffy. I can't get out of here on my own.''

Grammatica smiled and nodded. ''Yes-s-s-s.'' The tip of a forked green tongue flickered across his scaled lips.

Three hours later, still with a buzz in the back of my head like nothing I'd ever felt before—like being drunk but with crystalline speech and thoughts—I pushed my nose filters in place and ventured out from Grammatica's shop. The sun shone brightly through the haze, making the day as hot and sticky and unpleasant as possible. Dayworkers in gray suits and gray uniforms crowded the streets: no other animen or glitterfolk in sight this early, of course, just mindlessly conforming masses. I stopped and squinted a quick left-right, but found nothing out of the ordinary.

Deliberately, I shifted the small paper-wrapped package under my left arm and the stolen canister under my right to more comfortable positions. The package contained a hundred million newdollars, all in creased old nonsequential ten-thousands. Grammatica had taken the rest of the cash for his services and I hadn't argued, considering what he'd done, and the secrecy I needed. The canister held a dozen old vids, mainly for their weight. Pietr or his friends were certainly watching me leave, even if I couldn't see them, and I had to maintain the charade of still having the second PED in hand: an empty canister served as decoy.

It was Hangman who landed the aircar and popped the door for me. He'd been at my house when I called, and he'd left Jeffy sleeping to come get me.

I tossed both canister and cash onto the seat, then climbed after them. We lifted fast.

"How much?" he asked.

"A hundred million." I peeled back a corner of the paper so he could see the green of the bills. "You and Jeffy can split ninety; I took most of my share already. Or rather, Grammatica did."

"Fair?"

"Very," I said. "I feel like shit, though."

He laughed, not kindly.

I looked back to see a small red luxury coupe slip from one of the alleys adjacent to St. Jude Street. It gained altitude quickly, swinging around to follow us. Pietr? Pietr's friends?

It merely confirmed my suspicions; never trust a tech. Pietr wasn't willing to accept just one of the PEDs. Either that, or word of our theft had already leaked from his organization. We'd have to lie low for a while. But, with a hundred million left over from this job, we could afford it.

Hangman had seen the coupe too. He just sighed. No problem for him, I knew; we'd had aircars tailing us before, and he'd always managed to lose them.

Eight hundred meters up, we matched speed with southbound traffic. Buildings flowed below, an endless brick ocean. I watched the red coupe on the rear monitor. Its pilot kept back a discreet distance.

"Where?" Hangman asked.

"The harbor turbostation, I think." That would be the easiest place: lots of crowds, lots of confusion, lots of feet to guard innocent Sprawlers like me. I grinned and leaned back.

Hangman cruised for twenty minutes, letting the red coupe's driver relax and fall into the easy rhythms of flying. Then, without warning, he dropped us from the traffic flow like a falling stone—red lights blinked on, and the open-channel monitor shrilled with annoyed voices from drivers around us. But we'd done nothing illegal or even unusual. The red coupe, trapped by surrounding vehicles, was forced rapidly on.

The turbostation loomed before us. It resembled a Greek temple more than anything else, with twenty-meter-tall fluted marble columns on all sides. Statues on the roof showed all the Greek gods in scenes of travel: Zeus on a transit platform, Hermes in a two-seat aircar, Poseidon in an underwater tube-train, a whole pantheon of travelers.

Hangman coasted into the passenger-unloading zone. I got out, tucking the canister under one arm, and headed for the nearest entrance—walking fast but not too fast. I wanted the red coupe's driver to see me.

The coupe had just landed when I reached the doors. I glanced back and saw a pair of dogmen climbing out—both total huskies, with teeth that gleamed silver from steel implants. When they looked my way, I pushed through the door into the terminal.

The ceiling arched high overhead; to either side, stairs led down to the train platforms. Dozens of transit lines came together here, and hundreds of turbotrains left every hour.

The floor underfoot vibrated faintly from their passage. To the left, against the wall, stood rows of lockers.

I jogged to the nearest empty locker, stuffed the canister into it, and sealed it closed. Then I quick-keyed a credit number and left my handprint. It wouldn't open for anyone else as long as my account had cash to debit—at current rates, another thousand years or so.

A small gift shop stood a few paces down. Overhead, holos flickered through the brands of candy and gum and pocket-vids it carried. I could hide there easily enough. With a casualness that hurt, I strolled over and entered the shop.

As the smogguard staticked around me, I caught a glimpse of the two dogs bounding into the station. *Too late!* I thought triumphantly. *The drop's been made. I'm gone.*

I busied myself among the birthday cards, watching over the top of the rack as the dogs pushed through crowds. Finally they stopped and exchanged a few terse words. Splitting up, each took a different side of the station. They trotted down onto train platforms to search for me there.

Chuckling, I tossed back the card I'd been holding and left the shop. Slowly, carefully, as though I had all the time in the world, I headed back toward the unloading zone.

Hangman was still waiting in the passenger-unloading zone with the aircar. I climbed in beside him and locked my door.

"No trouble," I said.

He lifted wordlessly. When I twisted around in my seat, I noted the red coupe still sitting by the curb, empty. A pair of feet were writing a parking ticket for it while a third prepared to tow it away. I nudged Hangman and pointed that out. Face pressed against the window, I watched until the turbostation vanished behind skyscrapers.

Then Hangman handed me the vidphone. I could take the hint, so I dialed my house's number.

The 'phone rang ten times, then the house computer picked up. Kaleidoscoping patterns of light filled the viewscreen as a soft voice asked if I cared to leave a message.

"It's me," I said. "Jeffy—are you there? If so, pick up."

He didn't answer. The house computer, having analyzed my voice, said, "There are no new messages, master."

"Thanks," I said, and hung up.

It took perhaps another half hour to get to Fishtown. As we circled down, I stared at the deserted streets and wondered where Jeffy might be. Probably tranqued himself to sleep, I thought.

Finally we reached my house. Hangman cleared us through the defenses and made a perfect landing. He began powering down the aircar.

Yawning, head aching, I got out and stretched. I took a glance across my neighbors' houses, but as always found nothing out of the ordinary, not even a pigeon to break the monotony of tarred and antennaed rooftops.

Jeffy had the right idea, I thought. More than anything else I wanted to crawl into bed and sleep for a week myself. The PED had taken more out of me than I'd thought it would.

Crossing to the twin durasteel doors, I pressed my palm to the handpad. The computer chirped happily. The lift came and the doors opened with a hiss.

I started forward—then caught myself and stared in surprise.

The indicator lights across the back wall glowed red. Every single one of them.

Security breach! something inside me screamed, and I took a deep, calming breath to control myself. Slowly, painfully slowly, I turned and walked back toward the aircar. *Don't run. Don't let them know you know.* They had to be watching us, somewhere out there. I opened my door and slid in beside Hangman.

He looked up. "What?"

"Power up," I said quietly. "Security's down. This isn't a safe-house anymore."

He sent the aircar's repeller fields racing with power. Over our engine's roar, though, I heard a distant rising hum of sound. I bit my lip in anger and frustration.

And around us, on all sides, little red coupes rose from the street level. They closed in fast.

6

Hangman shoved the repellers to full power, and our air-car shot straight up. The red coupes rose after us, engines roaring. I counted seven of them. Their windows were screened, but somehow I knew they had dogs at their controls.

"Ground level," I told Hangman. "Get between buildings. We can lose them there."

Grunting, he accelerated, sliding us down toward the street. But fast as my aircar was, the coupes were faster still; they pulled alongside. When I craned my neck to see, I found another coming down on top of us. Radar warnings began to flash on the control panel, and the computer began automatic crash precautions. When it tried to take over steering, Hangman shut it down.

"Lower!" I cried.

"That's what they want," Hangman said.

The coupe to our left slid closer, so close I could have reached out and touched its side. It veered suddenly and struck us a glancing blow. Metal *scree*d on metal, and then we slid free again. Hangman cursed.

And abruptly our repeller fields cut out. We dropped nose-first like a two-ton steel brick. My stomach twisted, and I could feel my heart pounding in my throat. For an instant the world stopped. *We're dead*, I thought, pressing my eyes shut. I grabbed my seat, waiting for impact, certain we'd both be killed.

Then Hangman pushed the repeller fields back to full power. They whined in protest, but responded. Their sudden thrust crushed me back in my seat; I gasped for breath. We hurled skyward at a steep angle. For a second I saw the seven coupes ahead of us, all facing the wrong way, all starting to turn after us, and then they were gone and the universe did strange flip-flops. The street was *overhead*, I realized suddenly, and we were falling again—insanely, Hangman had turned the aircar upside down.

We rolled to the side and everything came up normal. Only my hands were shaking, and I could feel sweat trickling down my back and sides. I pulled deep shuddering breaths. How could he do something so stupid? Pressing my eyes shut, I tried not to vomit.

"You're crazy," I whispered. "You're going to kill us!"

"Better me than dogs."

He dived between buildings, down to ground level. Two turns and we were roaring down a tree-lined avenue. Branches overhead, thick with leaves, would hide us from the coupes. Even if the dogs saw us, they would hesitate to attack from above, through trees—the bottoms of their coupes weren't armored, and leaves could easily clog an aircar's repeller system.

But escape was too much to hope for. Before we'd gone half a block, two of the red coupes cut in from a side street. They powered down, completely blocking the way—we'd have to go back. But somehow I knew without looking that the dogs had cut off our retreat too.

"Have to run," Hangman said. "Hang on, Slash."

We landed hard, skidding on pavement. Our aircar slewed

to the side before coming to a halt. By then I had my door open; I rolled out and came up on all fours, in catform, running like my life depended on it. I didn't look back. I knew Hangman could more than take care of himself—and the dogs were after me, not him, in any case.

Luckily I spotted a gap between row houses, one of the thousands of little alleyways that honeycomb Fishtown. I tucked my head down and sprinted for it. Behind, I heard the coupes' doors opening and dog-voices shouting up the chase.

When I hit the alley, though, I couldn't hear them. A pleasant darkness enveloped me. This was my home, my true environment, and I knew I'd escaped. I let my eyes shift to nightsight, and abruptly the walls and trash-covered ground lit up in shades of pink and red. Ahead, more alleys joined in, became a maze. I recognized the corner; I'd been through here before and knew how to lose myself.

Two more turns and I reached a park, not the one with the wall where Jeffy had bragged his kill, but a smaller one faced with houses on every side. It had been landscaped in years long past, but the hedges had grown high and wild from neglect. I padded through them silently, confidently. A million interesting smells called for attention, and squirrels chittered from the trees—one of the few times I hated my heightened senses, my new instincts: too distracting.

Hundreds of cats had come through here within the last few days, and I felt sure the dogs would lose my scent: one set of synthetic skintights smells much like any other. And dogmen didn't really have the acute sense of smell a true canine possesses.

On the far side of the park I turned left and went as far as cover would take me. Through the hedge I could see another alleyway, one that led back toward the avenue. After a quick glance to make sure I couldn't be seen by the dogs, I dashed across an open stretch of ground into the alley. Then I headed back toward the aircars at a trot.

When I reached the avenue, the coupes were three blocks away. I studied them. Several dogmen, all total huskies like the ones who'd followed us to the turbostation, stood talking among themselves. Apparently they were waiting for the ones who'd gone after me, since they kept glancing nervously toward the alley I'd taken. Being in cat territory obviously bothered them, and with good cause. Had it been night, with cats out and about, they would certainly be dead or chased off by now. But unfortunately most catmen drowse away the daylight hours, preferring the cool, quiet night; I couldn't expect much help, unless a shadowcat patrol showed up.

So I just crouched there, tail lashing angrily, to watch and wait. They couldn't stay there forever, I knew.

I couldn't help but think of Jeffy. If he'd been there when the dogs broke into my house, he would have fought them, I knew. That was the way his mind worked. And considering the number of dogs involved, he certainly would have lost. Had they killed him, or merely roughed him enough to put him out of action?

If they hurt him . . . If they hurt him, I would go after their blood. A dozen teeth for a tooth, a hundred lives for his life. *Jeffy, Jeffy* . . .

A steady thrum of sound broke in on my thoughts. Aircars approaching fast, I thought. I peered up through the trees. It had to be shadowcats, too late to the rescue, as usual.

The dogs guarding the aircars also heard, of course. They let loose a series of howls for their companions. Another six dogs came tumbling from the alley at a run, tongues hanging out, panting like wolves. They bolted for their little red coupes.

Seconds later, three large, armored aircars crashed down through the trees, a typical shadowcat entrance. Branches shattered; leaves and splintered wood rained down. These aircars had no insignia or license numbers, but I knew them well enough: shadowcat troop transports. The shadowcats were Fishtown's private police force, with the emphasis on *force*.

Hatches popped. A dozen panthers swarmed from each aircar. Like all shadowcats, they were among the biggest catmen alive, their muscles ridiculously enhanced, their bones enlarged and strengthened—you didn't want to meet a shadowcat in the dark on a bad day. They could take out dogmen like the ones in the coupes blindfolded and hobbled. And if muscle wasn't enough, the belts around their middles held stunguns and accoustic grenades, too.

Hitting ground, they set off after the dogs, roaring their hate and anger. Several threw grenades, which exploded with deafening bangs. I winced and covered my ears.

But by then all the dogs had scrambled into their little red coupes. Overcharged repeller fields whining, they lifted just before the first shadowcats reached them. *Too late*. Rising swiftly, heading south, the coupes merged into the trafficflow and made good their escape. I watched until they vanished in the distance.

Only then did I emerge from my alleyway. Hangman appeared twenty meters down on the other side of the street. He'd also circled around and watched them go.

So much to do, I thought. I had to find Jeffy, make sure he was all right. Then I had to track down whoever had sicced the dogs on us. I couldn't let business partners turn me over to my enemies. For that I'd need more info on the dogs in the red coupes. This seemed the perfect excuse to try out my new toy—though I wished circumstances didn't force it.

"Black Rabbit," I whispered.

I felt an odd tingling behind my eyes, suddenly, and then I grew light-headed, as if all the blood had rushed from my brain. Abruptly the tingling stopped and I felt completely normal again. Had the PED worked?

I tried thinking back to the attack on my house, and the chase leaped to mind faster than I would have thought possible, and in greater detail. I discovered I could study any scene as though it were a picture. I could see why the dogs wanted the PEDs back. I examined Hangman, the aircars, my roof to the smallest detail—I could even count the bricks in the chimneys of neighboring houses. *Incredible*.

A hand clamped down on my shoulder. I blinked and found two of the shadowcats looming over me.

"You're coming with us," the one on the right said. His tone left no room for dispute, and his grip tightened painfully.

"Why?" I asked. "I didn't do anything."

"No trouble now," he said, voice sharp, and his hand dropped to the stungun at his belt. "You wouldn't want to resist arrest, would you?"

"No, no!" I said quickly, surrendering to the inevitable. "I'm a law-abiding citizen. I don't want any trouble!"

"Good," he said. His smile was too toothy. "I knew you'd want to cooperate."

I nodded reassuringly. I'd had a friend once who'd gotten on the bad side of a shadowcat. One day they picked him up, broke both his legs, and dumped him in dog territory. Luckily the dogs had taken pity on him and brought him to a bodyshop—but taking charity from *dogs* hurt almost as much as the wounds did.

I didn't want anything like that happening to me . . . either part. So I let the two shadowcats push me to the wall, lean me against it, spread my legs, and search me. They did it quickly and impersonally, confiscating my belt, pouch, and collar. They didn't offer a receipt; I didn't expect one. I didn't expect to see any of my belongings again.

They handcuffed me and led me back toward their aircars.

Perhaps it made them feel important, like they were doing their jobs. I'd get it sorted out soon enough.

But as we walked, they remained oddly quiet. When I asked, they refused to tell me who'd sent for them, why they'd arrested me, or where we were going. I found their silence increasingly annoying, but kept my feelings private. No sense provoking them further.

We skirted debris from the ruined trees, broken limbs and crushed branches mostly. This section of the avenue looked as if a hurricane had swept through.

The shadowcats had Hangman in custody too, I saw; like me, he knew better than to resist. He'd been handcuffed. As I watched, another pair of shadowcats bundled him into the first aircar.

As they led me to the second aircar, I asked, "Aren't you even going to tell me what all this is about?" in a small voice.

"Just following orders," the shadowcat said. He pushed me into the windowless rear compartment reserved for prisoners, then clicked the lock.

Orders? I didn't like the sound of that, and began pacing side to side, like a caged animal. If they'd been ordered to arrest me . . .

But that didn't make much sense. To arrest us, they'd have to know the dogs were after Hangman and me. And they'd have to know why. How could they know? Who could have told them about the PEDs?

I would have given quite a lot to hear what the shadowcats in the front compartment were saying. Unfortunately, the wall between us had been thoroughly soundproofed.

The aircar didn't lift for some time; perhaps the shadowcats were still combing the area, making sure all the dogs had gone. That was their job, after all—keeping Fishtown safe for catkind. Normally they kept a low profile; you could go months without seeing one. But you always knew they were out there somewhere, watching and waiting, keeping catkind safe.

Sitting in the dimly lit compartment, thinking about our arrest, I realized how little I really knew about the shadowcats. They were supposed to work for Hatter, the lion who ran Fishtown ("Mad Hatter," some called him, but never to his face). And I knew next to nothing about Hatter beyond his catshape. Hatter simply gave orders and people followed them because that was the way it had been as long as anyone could remember. And he had the shadowcats to back him. But where did his authority come from? Perhaps he had just seized it after the Crazy Years and he'd had the strength and authority to hang on all this time.

Which still didn't explain why the shadowcats had arrested me. "Just following orders," the shadowcats had said. Whose orders? Hatter's? What were they up to?

Perhaps they'd arrested me because I was there. Because they needed to bring someone in, to look like they were doing their jobs. Perhaps—but I doubted it. I'd never heard of the shadowcats arresting someone without cause. They worked too much in the background for that.

What if they know about the PEDs? I shook my head. *Impossible.*

Finally, we lifted. Our flight was short, no more than three minutes. I could guess our destination: Hatter's palace—his private underground complex in the center of Fishtown. It also housed the shadowcats' headquarters. I'd never been there before, and knew next to nothing about it—you didn't get in unless you had business with the shadowcats or Hatter, and I'd always avoided both.

When the engine powered down, a different pair of shadowcats opened the door to my compartment.

"Out," they said. When I didn't move fast enough, they grabbed my arms and jerked me from the aircar.

"No need to get rough," I said slowly, shaking my fur smooth. "I was coming!"

They relaxed a bit. That gave me time for a quick glance around.

We stood in a large hangar. Durasteel beams supported a concrete ceiling perhaps twenty meters overhead. Dozens of aircars, varying in size from small luxury models to troop transports like the ones the shadowcats had used to chase off the dogs, stood parked in tidy rows. Shadowcat mechanics worked on several. The hangar's entrance—huge and gaping, through which a muted sunlight shone—lay far to my left. Shadowcat guards stood duty there, energy rifles in hand. Of Hangman I saw not a sign.

The pair of shadowcats didn't give me time to see more. They hustled me into a side corridor that sloped sharply downward. Passing two more guards with energy rifles, we came to a lift. A car waited, and when I balked, they hauled me inside with little ceremony. It seemed I *would* go where they wanted me to, no matter what I thought about it.

The lift carried us down several levels, and at each I saw more armed shadowcats standing guard. Finally it stopped, and the shadowcats half dragged, half carried me out into what looked like an airlock. It cycled, and we found ourselves in a small dead-end corridor. Transparent plastiglass doors had been recessed into the walls every two meters.

They stopped before the first one, and I saw it was a cell. It held a bench that might serve as bed if you were desperate, a toilet, and a small vent in the ceiling—that was it.

"You're not going to put me in there, are you?" I said.

"For your own protection," one of the shadowcats said. He palmed the lock, and the door swung open.

"What about my handcuffs?" I protested, holding them up. "You can't just leave me here like this—"

They shoved me in. I stumbled, growling, but by the time I turned, the door had already slid shut and locked.

They turned and left. I watched, face pressed to the plastiglass door, until I was certain they weren't coming back. Then I dropped into catform, only to pace, frustrated. I hated losing control of situations, and I certainly had no control over this one.

"Hangman?" I shouted. "Can you hear me?" I could see into the cells opposite mine—both empty, but perhaps they'd put him into an adjoining one. I strained, but heard no reply. *Just as well*, I thought. It wouldn't have done much good to find him locked away too. But it certainly would've made me feel better.

I heaved my shoulder against the door as hard as I could. The plastiglass gave the tiniest bit, as I'd known it would, but ten of me couldn't have muscled through it. Still, it made me feel better to try.

Abruptly my shoulder ached. Rubbing it, I sat down on the bench. *I'm getting too old for this*.

I mopped my face and realized I was sweating heavily. It was too hot in my cell; the vent in the ceiling wasn't working. I rose and paced for a minute, but that didn't help, so finally I just lay down and tried to doze. That would be the best way to pass time.

But my thoughts were in turmoil, and I couldn't get comfortable. I kept thinking about my friends. Were they all right? What had the shadowcats done with Hangman? What had the dogs done with Jeffy?

Brooding, stomach knotting from hunger and worry, panting from the heat, I lay there for what must have been hours. I kept running through the events in my mind, trying to find some logic, some clue that would tell me about Jeffy. And I rehearsed what I'd say to the shadowcats when they returned. *Inhumane, torturously cruel treatment*. Even the feet give you a phone call. *But shadowcats aren't police. They aren't bound by the law when they don't want to be.*

Finally I heard a noise outside, the airlock cycling. I rolled off the bench to face the door.

Two shadowcats stood outside. This pair looked even larger and meaner than the ones who'd locked me in, and both held stunguns ready.

The larger of the two palmed the lock, and the door slid open. "Out," he said. A nasty-looking scar ran down his right cheek and across his mouth, puckering his cat-lips into a perpetual snarl. With bodyshops so fast and cheap, I realized he had to like the effect to keep that scar.

When he fingered his stungun as if he wanted to use it, I decided to obey him, and fast. I moved out of my cell as he'd ordered, quickly and quietly, trying to look as meek and cowed as I could.

The corridor's cooler air felt wonderful. I'd read somewhere that a hot room induces stress—probably deliberate in my case, I decided in retrospect, especially if they wanted to interrogate me.

"This way," the scar-faced shadowcat said, gesturing toward the airlock with his stungun.

I followed instructions. Back into the lift, down three more levels, through two more guard checkpoints, and then into a plushly furnished office. A bookcase filled the far wall. Before it stood a huge teak desk, and before the desk sat a single straight-backed wooden chair. The shadowcats pushed me into the chair and took up positions to either side and slightly behind.

I looked around as covertly as I could. Oil paintings decorated the walls, mostly studies of sunflowers. Van Goghs? I thought so, all doubtless originals. The place oozed culture and refinement, from the soft classical music in the background to the delicate hint of perfume in the air. And, good news, they obviously hadn't taken me here to torture me . . . though that could always come later, I thought.

Then the music stopped. After a pause long enough to

become uncomfortable, part of the bookcase swung back and Hatter himself walked in on all fours. He wore his lionform like a robe and his mane like a crown. And he was big, as big as his shadowcats, but where they were steel he was velvet: going to fat, slack-muscled, too plush from the good life. He had to be old; I'd heard of him as long as I could remember—twenty years, at least, with him ruling all Fishtown.

For a second he stared across the room with those piercing coal-black eyes, then he swept forward. He had a definite presence. You could feel it like electricity in the air. *Pheremones*, I thought suddenly. *He's putting them out like nobody I've ever met.* The shadowcats stiffened to attention behind me.

As he approached, Hatter stood on his hind legs and straightened, bones expanding or contracting as necessary until he stood on two feet in his humanest form. Slowly he sat on the corner of his desk, and only then did he look at me. His eyes were cunning. I shivered as his lips pulled back into a smile.

"So," he said, and his voice was as rich and mellifluous as science could make it, "I hear you had a bit of a run-in with dogs today, Mr. Carter. Or may I call you Slash?"

"You know me?" I asked, honestly surprised. I felt a tremor of apprehension.

"I know," he said slowly, "all of my people. But you— yes, I know you in particular, Slash. Twenty-two years ago, you went cat. Before that I understand you were an accountant, and as a child a common criminal. A thief, a brigand, an extortionist who worked the fringes of the Sprawl. And yes, perhaps you were even a murderer."

I winced with every word. Yet I couldn't deny it, because it was true—in my youth I had been all those things and worse, to my eternal disgust and embarrassment. My parents had been dayworkers who'd lost their jobs in the last great wave of mechanization. Out of work, on the public dole, they'd been forced down, down, down, crushed inexorably by a system that no longer wanted them or their kind. So I'd grown up among the streeters, run with gangs, savaged for sport and profit.

No luck in my escape from the streets: I was smart. By the time I was fourteen I ran things, made plans for my gang, did the brainwork to make our crimes safe.

But I also knew streetlife dead-ended; I just waited for the right moment to get out. Finally, when I was seventeen, we hit big, half a million from a liquor store. I grabbed and ran. My parents were dead by then, so I had nothing to lose.

First I bought a new face, a new identity, and new clothes; basic stuff. Then I accessed the NewsNets and went through reams of career opportunities. I was young and bright, with ready cash—just what people wanted.

Every call I made brought apprenticeship offers. I finally picked an accounting firm. Two years and I'd have a real job, and they would pay for night courses at college. What better choice? So I signed the papers and learned numbers and ended up spending ten years with them. At college I found a wife, and we had two children. It felt like heaven.

Everything shattered, though, when terrorist dogmen killed my family. It made me crazy for a while, sick inside from anger and despair. I gave up my job to pursue those dogmen. Dogs and cats were enemies, so I went cat.

In catkind I found allies like Hangman. We killed dogs, stole from them. My childhood with streeter gangs had prepared me; I had a talent for robbery, and it paid very, very well. My hatred had spred to all dogkind by now, and each scum dogman we killed made my pain more bearable.

"In running away," Hatter continued, "in going cat, you seem to have found a nobler pursuit. Even though you are still a parasite, you are an acceptable one here." He held up one golden paw before I could protest. His fingers were slender, perfect. "I know what you do. You annoy dogs. You steal little bits and pieces from them—drugs, technology, whatever they're dabbling in. It's harmless, as long as you stick to dogs. But this time you're in too deep. You took some devices, very special devices, and if you want to live through this, you're going to have to turn them over to me. I'm the only one who can save you, Slash."

"What about Hangman?"

"He's in protective custody for his own good. And I have your kit, too."

"Jeffy?" I asked, hope rising. "You have him here?"

"That's right. The dogs left him for dead. My shadowcats brought him in, and my surgeons revived him. They're fixing him up now."

"Thank you for that," I said.

"Now, the PEDs. Where have you hidden them?"

"I'm sorry," I said. "I wish I could give them to you, but I can't. They're already sold."

"I can get you a better deal than you'll get anywhere else. And I mean *anywhere*."

"I don't doubt it, but—"

At Hatter's nod, the shadowcat behind me pressed something against my neck. The next thing I knew, the world exploded in flashing lights and burning pain, *pain*, *pain* like nothing I'd ever felt before.

I screamed. I couldn't help it. The searing agony, the white-hot fire raging on and on through my body—

It stopped as quickly as it had started. I slumped in the chair, moaning, my insides so much jelly. I made fists, trying to stop my hands from shaking. I had a lump in my throat so large I couldn't swallow it away.

The scar-faced shadowcat had used his stungun, I realized. He grinned down at me. You're only supposed to tap someone with a stungun, but he'd pressed it in place and kept the electricity flowing. I moaned and began to shiver uncontrollably.

I blamed Hatter. He'd ordered it, and for that I could never forgive him. It was cruel, just as the heat in my prison cell had been cruel, and cruelty was one thing I would never abide. I swore then and there he'd never get anything from me, not a word, no matter what he did. Like Hangman and Jeffy, I'd been psychoscreened. Nothing could drag information from me, not drugs, not pain, *nothing*, if I didn't want to give it.

If I'd known it was coming, I could have blocked the stungun's pain, too, with the psychoscreening: that's why it's so effective against torture. Hatter must have known about my psychoscreening to resort to surprise shocks from a stungun so fast.

"Let's have a little bit of cooperation, shall we, Slash?" Hatter said, leaning close. I could smell his breath, hot and sickly sweet as perfume. "I need the PEDs. I need them very badly, more than you can imagine. And I'm going to get them."

"I don't *have* them!"

"But you can get them back, can't you?"

"No." I pulled myself upright, trying to hide my hate, trying to look as despairing as I could. I all but sobbed, "I sold them fast—through a middleman—I know hot equipment—that was the hottest—"

"Dear, dear, dear," Hatter said. He leaned back, tapping his chin with one claw. "That presents quite an inconvenience. And I must say it pretty much ends your usefulness to me."

"I'm sorry," I lied. "I'd give them to you if I had them. You know I would, Hatter. You're the boss!"

"If you can think of a way to get them back . . .?"

I shook my head. "They're out of the country by now. Korea, I think."

"A pity." He stood, gave a dismissive wave to the shadowcats behind me, and went to the bookcase. He paused there, looking back. His gaze cut like a knife. "Do let me know if you come up with anything useful, Slash."

He went through the hidden door. The bookcase closed up at once.

"Let's go," said the scar-faced shadowcat. He hauled me to my feet. Then he produced a key and unlocked my handcuffs.

I stared at him warily, rubbing my wrists. "Is this some sort of trick?" I asked. "I'm supposed to run and you're supposed to shoot me? Is that it?"

"Your audience is over; you're free to go. Perhaps you'd like to see your friends?"

"Yes," I said uneasily. "First my kit."

He gave a mocking half-bow and motioned me toward the door. "After you."

Too easy, I thought. Hatter wouldn't let me go so fast if he thought I might still be useful to him. Perhaps he intended to keep Jeffy and Hangman hostage until I produced the PEDs—just give me a quick look so I knew they were alive, then set me free to track down the equipment. I'd see. And I'd stay alert.

I led the way into the hall. From there scar-face escorted me up two levels, to another corridor. The air here held the faint touch of antiseptic, and my pulse quickened. Hadn't they said Jeffy was hurt? I had to see him, had to know.

Scar-face stopped before a door. "This is it."

"Jeffy?" Eagerly I pushed through. "Hey, Jeffy—"

I froze in disbelief. There were dogmen inside, a lot of them, all looking at me. They held stunguns. The antiseptic reek grew stronger, and I realized they were using it to mask their scent.

They can't be here, I thought impossibly, *they can't be in the heart of cat territory, in Hatter's palace—*

I whirled. Scar-face, still grinning, slammed the door. Distantly I heard it lock.

Dropping to all fours, shapeshifting, I faced the dogs as panther. Then I snarled, tail lashing, and tried to stare them down.

They just laughed. There were too many of them, at least a dozen, all modded big and powerful, and I could see they weren't afraid.

"Nice pussycat," said the dog nearest me, a total Doberman. He flicked his stungun's switch, and it hummed to life.

7

They advanced on me. Sighing, I just sat on my haunches and waited. I knew better than to offer any resistance. I didn't have Jeffy's youthful strength or Hangman's down-and-dirty fighting skills, and I didn't want to end up crippled or dead. I was too old and worth too much for that.

"Say the word," I said, "and you can have it."

"Arms," said the Doberman.

I held them out. Grinning, tongue hanging out the side of his mouth, the dog took a length of cord from his belt and looped it around my wrists several times, drawing it painfully tight. Then he yipped and pranced back, pulling me with him. The whole pack began to bark.

I closed my eyes and raised my psychoscreen barriers. If they went for my blood, I didn't want to feel it—no chances this time.

But the dogs seemed to be playing more than anything else. I let them pull me along. The Doberman seemed to be enjoying his triumph—if he could get off on tying up a cat, good for him. Somehow he felt clean compared to the Hatter and the shadowcats. His was an honest malice.

And with pain-blocks up, I scarcely felt anything. The universe seemed flat and lifeless.

I must have laughed a bit: the dogs suddenly shut up and looked at me. But the thought wouldn't go away: this whole scene resembled an episode from a bad vid. *Betrayed by Hatter and the shadowcats, captured by dogs. What could be next?* If I closed my eyes, perhaps I would wake and find it all a dream, vanished like phantoms by the morning light.

The Doberman said, "Time to go. Keep up. Try to run, and we'll drug you. Simple?"

"Sure," I said.

We went through another door, into a deserted corridor. Of course it was deserted, I thought—Hatter couldn't let catkind know he dealt with dogs. Fear and hate of dogmen had been drilled into us as long as I could remember. *Dogs kill cats. If you see a dog, run for your life. Don't let dogs catch you alone outside Fishtown!*

We came to a freight elevator, and all packed in. This close, the antiseptic smell was smothering. I longed for my nose filters—taken by the shadowcats along with everything else in my pouch.

The Doberman pulled a switch, and the car started slowly upward. Six floors later, the huge double-doors opened, revealing a private garage. Inside sat a pair of large black aircars with darkened windows. I'd expected more of the little red coupes. But perhaps the shadowcats had put out an alert and this was the only way the dogs could get here.

The Doberman popped a side hatch and motioned me in. I climbed the steps slowly. Just as I reached the top, one of the dogmen slapped a drugtab on my leg; I felt microneedles pierce my skin. Too late I shook the tab away. My calf felt like ice, and the numbness quickly spread through my foot and thigh.

"It's only a sleepeasy," the Doberman said. "Relax and

enjoy the ride, pussycat.'' He slammed the door shut, bolting it securely from the other side.

I'd used sleepeasies before. First my hands and feet would go cold and numb, then I'd get drowsy and pass out. I'd have a couple of minutes before it took full effect, perhaps five if I lay still and fought to stay awake.

I found the light switch. Fluore nts flickered to life in the ceiling panels.

They'd put me in a small cubicle with a padded floor. Jeffy lay to my right and Hangman lay to my left.

I hurried forward. Jeffy first—breathing deeply, thank God. He'd been cut up pretty bad, his leopard skintights shredded across back and shoulders, his ears mangled, his face red-lined from scratches. Whoever'd fixed him up had only handled the big problems, the chest and stomach; minor wounds and cosmetics had been left for another day. I peeled back one of Jeffy's eyelids. His pupil was too big and barely responded to the light. *Drugged*.

Hangman looked even worse: blood covered his skintights, matting his fur in huge clumps. But when I examined him closely, I discovered the blood wasn't his own. He must have put up quite a fight when the dogs came for him. And, like Jeffy, the dogs had drugged him to sleep.

I relaxed and sank down on the third wall's bench. They'd both live, that was the important thing right now. Escape could come later, when we were all up and awake.

My hands were already cool and my vision had started to darken around the edges, as though the world were receding around me. I stifled a yawn; not much time left. I lay down, ear pressed against the compartment's forward wall.

Distantly, I heard a rustling, squeaking noise as the dogs boarded and settled down for the ride. Then my eyes closed and I started to drop off.

I caught myself just in time. Seconds to go before I passed out, I knew. Deliberately, I focused all my hatred on Hatter.

How could he turn us over to *dogs*? It hurt, that betrayal. There were some things you needed to believe in, like the power of God or the lies of politicians. For me, Hatter had always been one of those things—the greatest cat, who worked solely for the good of catkind.

I vowed to kill Hatter then and there. I let the hatred well up inside me until I didn't have room for anything else. For a second the dark receded, but I knew the adrenaline rush would keep me sharp for only a few moments more.

The dogs began powering up their aircar's repeller fields. Over the rising hum, I could just hear them talking.

". . . think they'll be ready at nine tonight?" one of the dogs was saying.

"After the stink Rex made last time, Hatter'll make sure," said another.

I jumped a bit at that. Rex—I knew the name. He was leader of the dogs, Hatter's canine equivalent. Rex and Hatter working together? Suddenly my kidnapping started to make a horrible sort of sense. And I didn't like it one bit.

I fought to stay awake, straining to hear every word.

"Better be ready this time," the first dog growled. "The wife's expecting me home early tonight. It's her birthday, and I promised to take her to a show. If those damn cats make us late like they did last week—!"

"Pete's kid was sick," said a third dog. "Give him a break, already! Cats have problems, too, you know."

"Still, they could show a bit of courtesy and let us know what's going on."

And so much for the war with dogkind, I thought. From the way they talked, they were used to dealing with Hatter, were even old friends with some of the shadowcats. It astonished me that Hatter could get away with it. It astonished me more that he would even try.

I had a lot to consider, and didn't have time to figure it all out. Again darkness rose around me, and I could feel the chill of the sleepeasy in my chest, icing my heart. I took a final breath, and then the cold and the dark had me.

I dreamed of Iceland, of a wind so cold it cut to the bone. I was hunting in catform, racing between glaciers on the heels of a little black rabbit. He remained tantalizingly near, but always just out of reach. Once he looked back and his eyes were yellow, like Jeffy's.

We hit a plain, and there the rabbit slowed. All at once he turned to face me, fangs bared. *Fangs?* In slow motion, I tumbled to a stop.

He began to swell like a balloon, growing larger, changing shape. He eclipsed the sun, huge as the sky itself. Now a gigantic dog, he bent toward me, mouth open, teeth gleaming like new steel—

—and I woke, gasping for breath. For a second I didn't know where I was, then it all came back to me. *The dogs*—

I rolled over, eyes slitted, for a quick look-see. Jeffy, Hangman, and I lay in a small room on three cots. Diffuse lighting filtered through ceiling panels. The cell—if cell it was—had a durasteel door and no windows. The far corner held a sink, which dripped slowly.

Groaning, head aching from the sleepeasy, I stood. The room swayed, and I staggered to the door. The handpad didn't respond when I palmed it; locked from the outside, of course. I wasn't surprised.

I crossed to the sink, leaned on it while I got my balance. At least the dogs had shown a bit of compassion; the drugs had dehydrated me. We'd all need water.

When I pushed the tap, rusty water spewed out. I waited until it turned milky white, then washed out the greasy-looking cup as best I could.

I drank deeply. The water hit my stomach like a brick, and I suddenly vomited. Fortunately, I hadn't eaten in a day and had nothing in me but water. When my body finished its protests, I drank again, more slowly this time. Then I scrubbed my face and hands, and that helped more than anything else.

I refilled the cup and crossed back to Hangman. He groaned a bit when I eased him up and put the cup to his lips, but he sipped. When I laid him back, he opened his eyes and shook his head slowly, side to side, as though trying to figure something out.

"Sleepeasy?" he finally said.

"Yes. Do you remember the dogs?"

"On the avenue?"

I shook my head. "Who drugged you?"

"Shadowcats."

"Did they torture you?"

"No." He made a face. "I broke free and ran. Stupid."

I nodded slowly. It figured. Hatter was playing some game with us, letting me see the dogs, letting me know his shadowcats were working with them. But why? I'd missed something important somewhere.

I went back to the sink, refilled the cup, then went to Jeffy. He sat up with a start when I touched his shoulder. His eyes were bloodshot; he'd taken quite a beating. Confused, frightened, he stared at me.

"Where are we, Slash?" he asked. "The dogs—"

"They've got us all, I'm afraid." Quickly I outlined what had happened, from the attack on my house to Hatter's betrayal.

Hangman nodded now and then, but said nothing. His gaze traveled across the room, and I knew what he was thinking: *if we're prisoners, the room must be bugged.* I caught his eye and nodded a bit.

"So how do we get out?" Jeffy asked.

"Just wait," I said. "They obviously have something planned. They've gone to a lot of trouble to get us here. If they wanted to kill us, they would have done it while we were asleep—far easier.''

"Cat-thinking," Hangman said. "Dogs are different."

Before I could answer, the door clicked and swung open. Dogmen filled the corridor. Five of them filed in, all Dobermans like the ones who'd captured me, all armed with stunguns. They made a semicircle in front of the door, giving Hangman a wide berth, I noticed happily. He'd put up quite a fight against the shadowcats; these dogs weren't taking any chances.

"Out," the largest said.

"Certainly, certainly," I said, showing my hands, moving slowly so they would have no cause to panic. "We wouldn't dream of arguing."

They didn't bind our arms or handcuff us this time; between the aftereffects of the sleeptabs, our collective wounds, and the threat of stunguns, we really weren't up to much resistance.

Down the corridor, a left turn, then down another corridor; we seemed to be in a maze much like Hatter's palace. For a second I had a truly frightening thought—what if we really *were* still in Hatter's palace?—but I rapidly dismissed that idea. I could smell dogs here, the scent thick and heavy like an old den: no need to mask their scent with antiseptic this time. They were home.

Finally, we came to a huge double door. It opened silently as we approached, revealing an arena. Three tiers of seats rose in front and on the sides. Dogmen filled them, beagles and bassets, shepherds and setters, Dobermans and huskies —a dozen different breeds and mixes, all silently watching, waiting.

I stopped in the doorway, not liking the place at all. Then I caught the smell of blood hanging in the air, sickly sweet, coming from ahead.

"What the hell is *this*?" I demanded.

"Go on," the Doberman beside me said. "Rex wants to talk to you. He convened the whole Council of Dogs just for you." And then he grinned, tongue hanging, and prodded me with the barrel of his stungun.

No escape that way. So I took a deep breath, dropped into catform, and walked slowly into the arena with all the pride and seeming courage I could muster. If Rex were here, sitting in judgment, so be it. I'd give him nothing.

Sand crunched under my paws. Jeffy and Hangman followed me out into the arena—and it really *was* an arena. That faint, lingering scent of blood came from underfoot, from the freshly raked sand. Perhaps dogs used it for games of some kind. Had we been chosen as the next victims in some sort of blood sport?

A dazzling spotlight flicked on, found us, pinned us. I squinted into the glare—just waiting. I'd never had much respect for theatrics.

At last one of the seated dogs—a golden retriever—rose slowly and majestically. He raised a piece of paper before him and began to read with ponderous finality:

"The three modified catpersons who stand before us are accused of crimes against all dogkind. They have murdered. They have stolen. And they have worked at all times to oppress honest, hardworking dogs. Will anyone speak for them now?"

An absolute silence fell. I squinted across rows of dog-faces and found unreadable dark eyes, pink tongues hanging out, shiny black noses. None moved.

I ached to do something, *had* to act, so I took a step forward. "I want to talk!" I said. "Is this some sort of—"

"Silence!" the golden retriever snapped.

"I *demand*—"

"*Silence!*" he roared, and the guards by the door took a couple of steps forward.

I glanced over and found their stunguns ready. They weren't playing this time. Hangman and Jeffy tensed, but I stilled them with a small shake of my head.

The retriever continued, "You will have a chance to speak later, at the end of your trial."

Trial? "Very well," I said, and shut up. My tail twitched uneasily. Suddenly I wanted very badly to be far away from here.

Turning, the retriever looked at all the dogs around him, none of whom moved. More softly, he said: "Since none come forward in defense of the prisoners, and not a word has been said to their good all night, it comes to the question. The accused may now make a statement before the final say."

I stared, not knowing how to react. I hadn't expected a trial. I'd expected questioning, torture, and finally death. A trial seemed ludicrous, considering our position.

Beside me, Hangman began to laugh. Jeffy nervously joined in. I winced; that wouldn't help.

I took another step forward. "I have something to say!" I shouted. "This whole thing is absurd. You have no authority over us! If you have a complaint, make it to the feet, or to Hatter!"

"We are authorized," the retriever said patiently, "to try you for crimes against dogkind. We are the Council, appointed by Rex to protect and defend all dogs. Will you make a final statement or not?"

I didn't know what to do. Finally, I said, "No."

He went on. "The evidence has already been brought forth. All the dogs here are fair and honest, and they will now have their say. *Begin.*" He turned to the right, looking at the top of the row of dogs.

An ancient chihuahua rose slowly. "Guilty," he said.

The second, a Doberman, stood. "Guilty," he said.

And the rest followed suit, *guilty, guilty, guilty,* until every dog there had spoken. None would meet my gaze thereafter.

The retriever stood once more, looking sadly down on us. "You have been found guilty of your crimes against all dog-kind," he said. "Rex, may he live forever, will say your sentence."

He sat, and the collie next to him rose. This had to be Rex, I thought—a beautiful dog with long white-and-brown fur and a delicately crafted face. His eyes held the tired patience I'd once found only in grandparents, when grand-parents meant something in the world.

"It is with deep sorrow that I must pass this judgment," Rex said, voice so low I could scarcely hear. "It pains me to discover death—any death—in dogkind. That these three cats have chosen to make their living from murder makes their crimes all the more heinous. There can only be one punishment. I say this, then: tomorrow at dawn let them be shot dead by my guards. So be it."

He sat, and I stood there stunned. Hangman and Jeffy had stopped their laughing.

8

The guards escorted us back toward our cell. Jeffy shuffled his feet, looking shocked, and for once I found I didn't have much to say either. After they'd locked us in, I flopped on my cot and curled up to think.

Hangman drank, cupping water from the sink with his hands, then sat in the far corner and closed his eyes. He seemed unbothered by our trial. In fact, I thought as I watched through half-slitted eyes, he looked asleep. Perhaps he had the right idea; he had nothing to do at the moment. If we needed to make a break, best to have him fresh.

Jeffy began pacing, motions jerky and nervous. "Well?" he demanded after a minute of this, voice too high, too shrill. "What are we going to do, Slash?"

"Sleep," I told him. "It's been a long day, Jeffy. Get some rest."

"But Slash—"

"Do it!" I snapped.

He gave me a pouty look, but flopped onto his cot. There he tossed and turned uncomfortably. I knew he wouldn't get any rest, but having him cooled for the moment would give me think-time.

Nagging doubts about the trial first. Prime: why bother? If they wanted to execute a few cats, why not just kill them? Dogs had never bothered with formality before, as far as I knew. It was a waste of effort to drag us in just to announce our impending deaths. And: I'd never heard of any "Council of Dogs." If such a council truly existed, wouldn't I know of it?

I tugged my whiskers thoughtfully. Dogs never did anything without reason. Assuming a sham trial, where did that leave us? What had been accomplished, outside of terrifying Jeffy?

And suddenly I knew. They really *were* trying to scare us—and "they" included Hatter and his shadowcats. How better to do it than letting catkind's worst enemy, the dogs, play bad guy?

I took a mental step back and tried to see everything from a new angle. Hatter knew we'd all been psychoscreened. Physical torture couldn't pry the truth from us. But emotional torture—ah! No psychoscreening could prevent us from *caring* whether we lived or died. It would only keep us from feeling the pain of our executions.

Easy to prove one way or the other, I thought. *Just offer Hatter what he wants*. If he hoped for a desperate cat—one who'd do anything to survive, including betray friends and customers—I'd give it to him. At least for the present.

As Jeffy tossed again, I snapped, "You might as well relax. There's nothing we can do, so you might as well get used to it!"

Hangman said, "And perhaps they'll give us fish for our last meal, if we're lucky."

"How can you say that?" Jeffy cried. "They're going to kill us!"

"Could be worse," Hangman said.

"How?" Jeffy demanded.

"They could have shot us first and *then* put us on trial."

I rose. "Shut up, Hangman. I'm sick of your smug attitude. We're going to die, and it's all your fault!"

He looked at me blankly. "My fault? You're running things!"

"Sure, put all the blame on me!"

Jeffy moaned. "They're really going to do it. They're really going to kill us!"

"You knew the risks," Hangman told him. "So did Slash."

"Don't try to pin it on me!" I shouted. "It was your idea to go after those PEDs. We wouldn't be here today if we'd stuck to drug-runners!"

Then, pointedly, I took a slow glance around the room, mimicking the one Hangman had taken earlier. Subtext: *We're bugged, let's perform.*

Hangman nodded; no slack there. Only Jeffy didn't notice, but I couldn't do anything about it.

"It's too late to blame me," Hangman said. "We're all in this together."

I rose and began to pace angrily.

"Slash—" Jeffy began.

I cut him off with a sharp gesture. "You're just as bad!" I said. "Why did you have to kill those dogs? Huh?"

"Leave him alone!" Hangman said.

"Yeah," I sneered, though it felt like a knife inside me, "always sticking up for poor little Jeffy. I never should have adopted him—he's been nothing but trouble. I bet he's the one who told the dogs we'd taken the PEDs to begin with!"

Jeffy howled a bit and turned his head away. My insides knotted as I thought of what he must be feeling, the savageness of my betrayal. I longed to go to him, to explain—but couldn't.

Then I heard the door unlocking. I whirled. Hangman struggled to his feet.

A dog stepped in, not a doberman but a wolfhound this time. He held a stungun like an old pro. Little sparks of electricity jumped across its barrel: fully powered.

"Perhaps I can help you," he said, looking at me. "My name is Eden, and I represented you at your trial."

"What do you mean?" I demanded suspiciously. Deep inside I wanted to shout my triumph. I'd read the setup, dead cert.

Eden said, "It just might be possible to arrange a pardon for you and your friends . . . maybe. If Rex knew you were truly repentant for what you'd done."

"I am!" I said. "It wasn't my fault—I never touched those dogs—"

"Shut up, Slash!" Hangman growled.

"Go on," I begged the dogman. "Ignore him."

"You intercepted a high-tech shipment of ours. Heads, you know the ones. We want them back."

I let myself wilt. "But they're gone!"

"Where?"

"Don't tell him, Slash!" Hangman said, a dangerous edge to his voice. "You can't trust dogs!"

"You have my word," Eden said smoothly. "If you cooperate, Rex may well pardon you."

I looked at Hangman. "If there's any chance—"

"No!" he said explosively. He shifted to catform, growling deep in his throat.

Eden clearly knew what Hangman was capable of; he took a quick step back and held his stungun ready. It crackled with electricity.

"Get away from him, Slash," Hangman said, very sharp, very cold, in his best killer voice. "We don't deal with dogs."

"Fuck off," I told Hangman.

Roaring, he leaped for my throat. I had a horrible feeling he hadn't caught on after all, that he really meant to kill me.

As I stumbled backward, Eden stepped close and tapped Hangman's side with the stungun. I heard a short *zzzt!* and suddenly Hangman sprawled at my feet, twitching faintly, hair bristling like a porcupine's from the charge that had run through him.

Jeffy launched himself at Eden's back. It hurt me more than ever, but I cuffed him down. He cowered at my feet. I'd never struck him before, never laid a paw on him in the six years we'd been together. It hurt.

"Slash," he whimpered. *"Why?"*

"Don't be stupid, Jeffy. If we can get pardons—"

"That's right," Eden said encouragingly. "Surely your lives are worth a little information."

Hangman stirred, tried to stand. Eden jumped back. "Perhaps we should talk someplace more private," he said to me. "What do you say, Slash? Just us?"

"Sure," I said.

I went out first. More dogs waited in the hall, all Dobermans, all armed with stunguns. I raised my hands to show I meant no harm, slow, so slow. No sense getting shot by a nerved dog.

Eden followed. As the door slid shut, I saw Jeffy crouched over Hangman's body, gazing up at me with a betrayed, horrified expression. It made me ache inside, but I looked away, refused to meet his eyes. He must continue to think I'd turned on them. Our captors would still be watching the cell, listening to everything he and Hangman said.

"This way." Eden touched my arm.

Meekly I followed him to another room, this one furnished with table and chairs. We sat face-to-face. Eden put his stungun away and set a little recorder between us, which he activated with a flick of his thumb.

He didn't waste a second. "Tell me what happened after you ambushed the dogs at the dock," he said. "Leave nothing out. What seems like an inconsequential detail may be what we want."

"What about those pardons?" I said slowly.

"Let's hear some of your story first. Then we'll talk about pardons."

So I took a deep breath and launched into a rambling, unfocused tale of what had happened, with plenty of digressions and asides. Stealing the heads, fleeing to a bodyshop, getting fixed up, Jeffy bragging his kill . . . the next day finding a middleman, arranging a drop, and getting chased to the turbostation by dogs in little red coupes.

When I began to stray from the truth and Eden made no objection or comment, I realized he knew nothing about Grammatica, Pietr, the dogs who'd followed us to the turbostation, or the attack on my house in Fishtown. Very odd, but certainly no odder than anything else that had happened. I could only come to one conclusion, and that shook me: he belonged to a second group of dogs, one allied with Hatter and the shadowcats. The huskies in the red coupes were working for someone else.

Then how does he know about the PEDs?

I stopped after the chase at the turbostation. I'd given enough for free.

"About those pardons?" I asked.

"Guaranteed," he said quickly, eagerly. "Your story is exactly what Rex wanted. Go on, Slash."

"So after we lost the dogs at the turbostation, we went to the rendezvous point—lightning statue, near the north city hall. Two more dogs were waiting for us there. They gave me a hundred million, cash, for the PEDs—more money than I'd seen in quite a while."

Eden winced at the price. "They were worth a thousand times that much."

"How was I supposed to know?"

"What sort of dogs were they?"

"Big ones. You know, half Doberman, half husky—like the two from the turbostation. But definitely not the same ones, though they had a little red coupe, too."

"Where did they go?"

"They said something about Korea, I think? But that doesn't explain why they attacked my house this morning—"

"Thank you, Slash." Eden picked up the recorder and thumbed it off. Standing, he headed for the door.

"Hey—" I called. "What about me?"

"Wait here. Someone will return with the paperwork you need."

The door slid shut. I listened, but didn't hear it lock. Somehow, I wasn't surprised. I'd always prided myself on being fast on the pickup.

Time crawled as I counted seconds. When five minutes had passed (long enough for the dogs to clear the corridors), I rose. We were supposed to escape, I thought, and make it easy for the dogs: no complications, no mess, no bodies to dispose of. And we'd had the fear of Rex and his council thrown into us to keep us honest. Oh yes, these were clever doggies. My lip pulled back in a snarl. I'd take care of them after I took care of Hatter.

Time up, I stood and tried the door. Open, of course. I poked my head out cautiously. And of course the corridor was deserted.

I hurried back the way Eden had brought me, toward our cell. I didn't want to give Rex time to reconsider our escape.

The whole building seemed empty; I saw not a trace of a dog anywhere. Finally I pulled up before our cell. It had a lockpad, I saw, and a shiver went down my back. Lockpads used handprints like keys, and mine certainly wouldn't open it.

But I had nothing to lose, so I palmed it anyway. Perhaps

Rex and Eden had taken care of it after all—they'd managed everything else so far.

Ten seconds later, the lock clicked—operated remotely, I decided. It never should have recognized my palmprint.

Hangman and Jeffy stood waiting. Jeffy sighed in relief when he saw me, then took a hesitant step.

"Doubletime it," I said. "We've got to get out fast."

"Right," Hangman said, dropping to catform.

Jeffy said, "I knew you'd rescue us!"

"Save it!"

We ran. Two corridors farther, we found emergency stairs. We bounded up three at a time, me leading, Jeffy at my heels, Hangman as rear guard. The door at the top of the stairs said an alarm would ring when it opened, but I pushed through anyway. I didn't hear a sound; probably disconnected.

We emerged onto a rooftop parking lot. I gazed out across rows of small, personal aircars and saw not a trace of a dog.

The breeze carried the sweet, rich scents of grass and trees and growing things—certainly not the usual centerSprawl mix. The day felt cooler, crisper, than usual. We had to be north of Fishtown, I decided, somewhere in the upper fringe of the east coast civilization.

"New England?" Hangman said.

"Probably."

"What's going on?" Jeffy asked, sounding completely lost. "Why did they let us escape?"

The dogs couldn't very well evesdrop here, so I said, "It was all a setup to get info. I don't quite know what's going on, but it seems there are two groups after the PEDs—the dogs we stole them from, and Hatter and Rex, who seem to be working together. We'll have to watch catkind from now on, too."

"Interesting," Hangman mused.

"PEDs?" Jeffy asked, eyes wide. "What're they?"

"Best if you don't know too much about them," I said. "They're what the smugglers had in those canisters."

The dogs had certainly done their best to make our escape easy. Not that I trusted them yet—they could still swoop down on us at any moment, if they wanted. And I knew without a doubt that they still had us under surveillance. They'd be fools not to, and Rex and Hatter certainly weren't fools.

I waved Jeffy and Hangman forward. "Check the aircars. See if there's one with an ignition cube."

"Yes, sir!" Jeffy said, and sprang forward eagerly. Hangman followed right on his heels. They split up and headed down different rows, peering in through the windows.

Turning, I took a quick survey of neighboring buildings, looking for landmarks, looking for dogs. I recognized nothing. And, of course, the dogs kept themselves under cover.

Hangman whistled and waved. He and Jeffy had found an aircar, a black four-seater that had seen better decades. I trotted over, looked inside, and saw its power cube lying on the driver's seat.

"That's the only one," Jeffy called, finishing his search and trotting over.

"No wonder," I said. "Nobody would want to steal *this*!"

"Get in," Hangman said. He opened the driver's door and slid behind the controls.

I got in on the other side. The control panel was cracked and dirty, and half the gauges didn't work, but the repeller fields hummed to life when Hangman shoved the cube into place.

I activated the onboard computer and called up a map. Satellites gave our location: Pixel, Vermont. That would do for the moment. A couple of hours and we'd be back in the Sprawl.

Hangman lifted. My stomach lurched as the repeller fields sputtered for a second.

At a sedate crawl, we headed for the southbound traffic-flow. I didn't think this aircar capable of much speed and upgraded our flight time to three, maybe four hours.

I leaned back, put my feet up, and smiled. Things were certainly looking better.

Then Hangman announced, "We're being followed."

9

I turned one of the rear monitors. A dozen aircars trailed us at various distances, most just heading in the same general direction, I knew. All had darkened windows; all had real-looking license numbers and registration marks. Nothing particularly suspicious stood out.

"Which one?" I asked.

"Black sedan, three back."

I recognized the model: a sporty ten-seater with an over-powered engine, fast and strong but too wide on turns. I'd almost bought one once, when I still had delusions of the glamorous life-styles of those who stole for a living. When I ran estimates on maintenance and fuel, though, it was enough to put me off luxury cars for life. These days I would never have considered one: too flashy. Much better to be quiet, subtle, and safe. Dogs would probably never realize that simple fact.

Jeffy was craning around the back window, trying to see it. "But I thought—"

I said, "I should have realized they wouldn't let us skip

so easily. They need to make sure my story's legit. So they're going to follow us until something happens, and hope we lead them to the PEDs. Damn nuisance.''

"Destination?" Hangman asked.

"Nearest turbostation, I think.'' I turned the monitor so he could see it again. "This is a stolen aircar, don't forget. The sooner we ditch it, the better I'll feel.''

"Lose them first?"

"If you want.''

Grinning toothily, Hangman focused his full attention on the controls. We dropped to a different level, this one heading for the center of Pixel, and slowly accelerated. The sedan continued to trail us at a discreet distance.

As we neared city center and traffic increased, Hangman upped speed, darting among other aircars as though through an obstacle course. We cut within centimeters of an old white cruiser, then a transit platform, then a delivery truck. The open channel squealed with protests, and the truck driver cursed us back through three generations.

Hangman didn't bother to reply. He brought us lower still, roaring between buildings, scarcely ten meters above ground. Pedestrians scattered. We banked through a turn, then turned again, accelerated all the while. Our repellers started a slow whine as they began to overheat, and suddenly our aircar began to shimmy. But Hangman wouldn't let up, continued to push for more.

The sedan lost all pretense of hiding and rifled after us, closing fast. I tensed, claws rippling from my fingertips. They'd try to bring us down, I thought, try to capture us once more. This time I wouldn't give up without a fight. Even if their aircar outclassed ours, even if they outnumbered us ten to one, even if they outgunned us, I still wouldn't let them take me back. I wouldn't stand before Rex again as a prisoner. Pride, yes, I still had that; but it went beyond the personal. It involved something else, something important, something primal. I remembered Jeffy bragging his kill on the wall what seemed years ago, and then it seemed to me the very nature of catkind must lie at stake. To stop now, to give in to dogs, would mean surrendering something important. Perhaps cat-kind's freedom.

A warning light on the control panel began to blink. I stared at it, surprised. Radar? I pressed up to the side window, looking for its source. If the feet had a speed trap . . .

Hangman laughed and kept our crazy pace. The sedan's driver hesitated, began to fall behind, then panicked and pushed his speed to catch up.

When I realized what Hangman was doing, I grinned. *Got you,* I thought to the dogs.

As if on cue, a huge black aircar with flashing lights on roof and underside cut in from a side street. Sirens shrilling, it pulled alongside the sedan. I could see half a dozen uni-formed feet in the aircar, all motioning for the sedan to land. The dogs complied.

Chuckling, Hangman turned the corner and slowed. No sense attracting further attention to ourselves. Of course, the feet had gotten our license number too, but I doubted it had been reported stolen yet. So the real owner would get a ticket faxed to him. *May it be Rex,* I thought.

"How did you know they'd stop the dogs instead of us?" Jeffy demanded.

"They always stop flashy cars first," I said. "The feet resent the megarich, same as everybody else."

Hangman grunted, "Predictable."

By then we'd reached the turbostation, done all in art deco style. Fountains splashed in front; everything, from doorways to windows, seemed tall and narrow and cast in shades of turquoise.

Hangman angled us down. Here, outside the Sprawl, space wasn't at a premium; they had a free parking lot for aircars. We could abandon ours with a minimum of fuss.

Easy, I thought smugly. But then, we were entitled to some luck for a change.

Paranoia still had the better of me: I bought continental passes from the vending booth, quick-keying my credit account. For the next month we'd be able to go anywhere in North America without buying another ticket, and so our movements couldn't be traced. Then I withdrew two hundred thousand in crisp thousand-dollar bills: pocket money for any purchases we'd need in the next few days. If my accounts were being monitored (entirely possible, and entirely likely), I didn't want to give any information away as to our movements. We'd pay up front for everything until the excitement died down.

I gave half the money to Hangman and tucked the rest away myself; no sense in one of us carrying it all. Then I passed out transit passes.

"Walk on two legs," I said, standing and trying to look as human as possible. They complied, Hangman like it was a duty, Jeffy with a kit's speed and enthusiasm. *Easier to blend in that way*. Who in a turbostation would remember three catmen among the tens of thousands of passengers through here every day?

"Back to the Sprawl?" Jeffy asked as we walked slowly and calmly for the boarding platform. *Typical commuters, we; no need to attract attention, no need to hurry or panic*.

"Why not?" I shrugged. "It's easy to hide in sixty-five million people. They'll never find us in the Sprawl if we don't want to be found." *And that will give us time to plan our actions, to decide where we want to go, and for how long*.

We boarded the first southbound train that came.

An hour and a half later, we pulled into a centerSprawl stop. It hadn't been the first we'd come to, nor the last on the line. I decided it would do and rose quickly, dropping to cat. Jeffy and Hangman tagged at my heels as I went out onto the platform.

The feet hadn't cleared out this turbostation in a while, and it seethed with humanity at its worst: streeters living in corners, harried-looking dayworkers scurrying on errands, knots of bored-looking people around dice games or food carts or vid displays. It was a zoo, stinking from the grease and charcoal smoke from the vendors, from the sweat and piss and accumulated odors of a great unwashed mass of humanity, from all the drugs and chemicals people used in this part of the world. Of course, nobody blinked as three catmen joined the noise and claustrophobic squalor. Why should they? We were the least memorable people here.

Longing for my nose filters, breathing through my mouth, I led Hangman and Jeffy toward the exit. A pack of screaming children in sequined rags skidded to a halt in front of me, lost in some streeter game, so I pulled back my ears and hissed at them. Grudgingly, they made way.

The exit read: 1544th Street. Good enough; I took it, hurrying up the steps.

Hot, humid air hit me like a physical blow when I passed through the smogguard. I gagged on exhaust fumes and chemicals; my eyes teared and my throat began to burn. An acrid, metallic taste filled my mouth.

This was the worst I'd ever seen the Sprawl. I fought my impulse to duck back into the turbostation—at least the air there had been breathable—and forced myself to look around.

Low, dark clouds shrouded the tops of skyscrapers, and a blanket of haze lay across the street. I couldn't see more than twenty meters in any direction. Bits of red and blue neon glowed like bruises in the distance, and banks of smog rolled down streets like waves on a beach.

Lockup weather, honest folk called it. When pollution settled over the Sprawl, when it grew so dark and thick you couldn't see your hand in front of your face, the streeters and glitterfolk ran wild, smashing, destroying, looting in a wild frenzy of violence.

I squinted up at the sky. Late afternoon; not much daylight left. We hoped we'd be gone before trouble started. If not, we could probably pass, since we weren't straight humans . . . but no sense taking chances.

"Hardware first," I said. "I feel naked without a pocket computer." *And nose filters first opportunity*, I silently added, cursing the shadowcats for taking mine.

"There's a 'phone on the corner," Jeffy said, pointing.

The three of us padded over to its little kiosk. Its smogguard wasn't working, so we pulled the glass doors shut and sat inside. Clean air hissed from vents in the floor. I took deep breaths, much relieved.

"Can I help you?" the telephone computer asked in a soft, feminine voice.

"Yellow pages," I said, "and a street map." I fed a thousand-dollar bill into the slot.

"Certainly, citizen." The directory flashed onto the screen. I began skimming entries.

The nearest computer store turned out to be a Tech-Tack-Toe two blocks over and one block down, on 1542nd Street. Tech-Tack-Toes mostly sold generics to glitterfolk, so I knew they'd be open as late as possible, even in lockup weather. You could get everything from computers to glow-in-the-dark feathers there. Overpriced, of course; but then, glitterfolk spent money like water.

I took a moment to scan for nearby hotels and transit platform stops, then tabbed off the computer and collected nine hundred and twelve dollars change.

We set off for the Tech-Tack-Toe. Night was just edging on, but stores had already started closing. All up and down the street, durasteel screens began sliding across windows and doors. *Lockup weather*. The merchants knew what was coming, could taste it in the air.

And the first of the glitterfolk had appeared too: youngsters eight or ten years old, fresh from school. They stood in the mouths of alleys, decked in cheap skinpaints and neon sparklers. Striking poses for each other, strutting with ponderous dignity, they tried to emulate their elders. Several threw back their heads and howled. It was a savage, primitive sound that made the hackles rise on my neck.

I took a quick glance at Jeffy and found him gaping at the glitterchildren. I'd let him live as sheltered a life as I could, and I realized he probably hadn't seen glitterchildren this close. Even before I'd adopted him, when he'd run with a gang of streeter kids, he would have avoided glitterfolk. Streeters keep their own company.

"Don't stare," I told him. "It's rude."

He looked at me, still wide-eyed. "I just—"

"I know," I said quietly. "But with the dark and the smog and the smell of fear everywhere, they're working themselves up for trouble. They *want* to hurt people. Glitterchildren might not know enough to leave cats alone. So we ignore them and don't attract their attention by catching their eyes. Got it?"

"Sure," he said, and concentrated on the pavement. "No problem, Slash."

Farther ahead, glitterchildren began dancing out in front of rolling landcars, laughing and taunting. When drivers honked and skirted them, they shouted insults, threw plastic bottles and broken bits of pavement. *Lockup weather*. Oh, yes, violence was coming fast.

Not that these glitterchildren particularly worried me; with our steel claws and fangs, we could more than take care of ourselves. Besides, they seemed to be leaving pedestrians strictly alone, concentrating instead on landcar harassment.

But you still didn't look, didn't invite trouble.

I quickened my pace. We'd have to hurry if we were going to find the store open. Even Tech-Tack-Toes would shut their doors rather than risk being burned and looted in a riot. They just stayed open as long as they could to squeeze the last 'dollar out of the last customer.

We rounded the corner onto 1542nd Street. This whole block seemed devoted to servicing glitterfolk. I counted no fewer than fifteen meatshops—humanoform boutiques where standard humans could get upgrades, from electric-powered glitterhair to tinsel eyes to new internal organs. One even had a sign in the window saying:

HUMAN KIDNEYS WANTED!!
Live Donors Only
→ No Synthetics! ←
Also: *Eyes, Teeth,* and *Livers*
Highest Prices Paid!

I shivered. Somehow, traffic in human organs always seemed sleazy, unlike animal enhancements in shops like Grammatica's. Perhaps it was a matter of perspective, the difference between selling parts of your original body and adding enhancements to it.

At the next alley, it seemed almost as if we'd passed some invisible territory marker. No glitterchildren here; instead, dozens of sullen, dirty faces peered out at us: streeters, massed and waiting for some signal only they would know. Their eyes were dull, tranqued, and they swayed to the intricate rhythms of musicjacks in their heads. I could feel their hunger, their pent-up hates and frustrations directed at a society that forced them to live in the streets like animals, all radiating like heat from a white-hot fire. Beside me, Jeffy was shivering. He refused to look the streeters' way, refused to acknowledge their existence.

Then, finally, we came to the Tech-Tack-Toe. When we

paused to look in the display window, lasers locked onto our retinas and began flashing prices. Holograms popped up around us, mostly glitterdressed models showing off the best and brightest the store had to offer. I ducked around a pair of holoed men made up as giant peacocks, huge fans of electrified tailfeathers spread behind them, and found myself in the doorway. Static cracked as we passed through the smogguard.

This Tech-Tack-Toe was the smallest I'd ever seen, a cramped little store so overstuffed with merchandise you could scarcely move. Racks and bins lined the walls from floor to ceiling, and boxes had been stacked in the center of the room, leaving tiny aisles to either side. No room for holos or displays of any kind in here; you had to know what you were after, or browse through everything.

I eased past clusters of glitterfolk examining radar scramblers, descramblers, electric stunguns, and microknives; carefully skirted bins filled with tubes of glitterpaint in a thousand bright colors; ducked under hanging displays of bird wings and feathers.

Computers lay at the very back of the store, in a recessed alcove. When we entered, a woman with transparent skin approached at once. I'd never seen her mods before, and stared more than was really polite at the blood pulsing through her veins and arteries, the intricate flexings of her every muscle, the little globules of yellow-gray fat that fleshed out her sparse frame. Lips painted bright red, eyebrows sketched in dark pencil, hair like spun platinum tied back in little coils with clear plastic bows—she looked more like a mannequin than a human. The name tag on her gray frock said, "Sapphire."

"Can I help you, gentlecats?" she asked. Her voice was husky. Copper filaments in her corneas flared with each word.

"Please," I said. "I need a computer." I caught a whiff of her then: she had on some pheromone-laden perfume, and

I felt a stirring in my crotch. I tried to suppress my body's lusts, and shifted uncomfortably; no matter how far you went from humanity in an animalform body, you couldn't escape your hormonal heritage, it seemed. I wanted her badly.

She smiled. "Are you here for the sale on our new Cray Microcomp XIV? It's on sale this week. Twenty-five giga-bytes storage per machine, interlaced with—"

"Afraid not," I said, easing foot-to-foot. "I need a new pocket computer." Quickly I outlined the programming I wanted: something to analyze small systems like those in aircars, and something to find bugs and tracers.

"Just the thing, gentlecat. This way, please." With a little giggle, she turned and swayed toward the back of the store. Her every movement seemed a work of art. Jeffy and I followed like cats in heat; Hangman came last, with more dignity than either Jeffy or I managed.

She brought us to a small display. I gave a little mew of delight, for there on a little pedestal sat a Hudson-Smith 242TX, Deluxe Pocket Model, exactly like the one the sha-dowcats had stolen from me. I picked it up lovingly, flipping back the control panel. Sure enough, it had all the standard jacks and processors: everything I needed in one compact unit. Easy. They'd stopped making this particular model at least a year before, so it was a blessing to find one.

"I'll take it!" I said.

"Cash, or debit account?"

"Cash."

She read its price tag, fed information into a wrist register, and said, "That model's on discount, so it comes to sixty-four thousand and thirty, with tax."

I counted out exact change, then watched as she carried it off to the register. *Perfection indeed*, I thought, watching her hips and shoulders, the intricate workings of her muscles. I sighed. I'd even begun to find her transparent skin attractive.

Untabbing my skintights at the throat, I tucked the computer into the hidden pocket under my left arm. Its bulge hardly showed.

"Your receipt," Sapphire said.

"Thanks." I accepted it.

I would've said more to her, but Hangman took my arm and pulled me back toward the front of the store. "Enough," he said. I just sighed again.

Outside, Hangman stopped. "We need a plan," he said. "Computer's fine. But what now?"

I gazed up the street. It had grown dark; the smog, thick by any standard, now seemed an impenetrable blanket across the city. I could scarcely see the Tech-Tack-Toe's neon signs overhead, and no lasers managed to lock onto our eyes or bring up holos.

"Things are too hot here," I said slowly. "I don't like messing with shadowcats *and* two sets of dogs. I figured we would spend the night here, pick up whatever else we want in the morning, then head north. Maybe try one of the Canadian states. Quebec?"

"I don't like running," Hangman said. "If they chase you away, you'll never get back. I'm not leaving."

"It's just temporary."

He shook his head. "There's a safe house in Fishtown."

"Whose?"

"Mine."

That stopped me. "An interesting idea," I mused, running through all the possibilities Fishtown presented. I certainly wouldn't mind hiding out in home territory. It was the last place anybody would look for us. And if Hangman said it was safe, I didn't doubt its security.

I agreed to go back. "But," I said, "the shadowcats are going to be searching for us, and enough people know what we look like by now that I don't want to take chances. We'll need disguises."

"Easy," he said. He padded back into the Tech-Tack-Toe. A moment later, he emerged with three tubes of black glitterpaint.

The siren over our heads gave a quick blast of sound. Jeffy jumped as if he'd been stuck with a pin, coming down on all fours in a wild panic.

"Calm down," I said. "They're just closing."

Steel screens rolled over the windows. The siren shrilled again, two long wails: closing fast. They probably had reports of riots starting farther up 1542nd.

Glitterfolk flooded from shops' doors, which then closed and sealed. The neon signs shut off and retracted into the building front; a durasteel screen slid over them. With signs and lights off, the building vanished into the smog. I literally couldn't see it anymore.

The glitterfolk who'd been shopping inside seemed in unusually good moods. They surrounded Jeffy and Hangman and me at once, laughing and joking. Their shimmering silver hair, their glittering neon-lit masks, their clothes that flashed red-yellow-green in intricate patterns—it all threatened to overwhelm. I took a quick step back and found myself treading on someone's toes.

"Beg your pardon," I said, turning.

The woman behind me spread her glowing orange feathers and cackled happily. A dozen electric eyes flashed on-off, on-off on her cheeks and face. "Nada, man," she said.

"Going glitter, pussycats?" someone called. I turned and squinted, getting the impression of a skeleton done all in silver and gold thread. Hard to see in the haze.

Of course, I thought, *they saw Hangman buying glitterpaint*.

"Just a bit of glitter," I said to the skeleton. "We thought we'd look good in shiny black tonight. What do you think?"

"This is the time for it!" the feathered woman called, and let out a long, whooping cry.

"Let us," another woman said, and scooped the paint from Hangman's grasp before he could protest.

Then they were all over us, gently rolling us over, spraying the glitterpaint onto our bellies and backs and rubbing it into our fur by hand.

Jeffy yowled.

"Quiet!" I told him. "They're doing us a favor."

It didn't take the glitterfolk long to finish. When they stood back, a man done in mirrors from skin to eyes to clothes waddled forward. I examined my reflection in his chest, turning this way and that, admiring my new look: the glitterpaint left me a brilliant black . . . not matte as a panther normally would be, but shiny black like wet paint. An interesting effect, indeed. One of the glitterfolk must have had a tube of white paint as well, since I now sported Indian war-paint stripes along my cheek-fur and down the bridge of my nose.

I looked at Hangman and Jeffy and found I scarcely knew them. *Excellent.* Nobody would recognize us in Fishtown. We might even start a new fashion trend.

"Thanks," I told the glitterfolk, really meaning it.

"Hey, pussycat," the skeleton said to Jeffy, "what're the new earmods for, hey?"

That set off inner alarms. Earmods? I hadn't had Grammatica do Jeffy's ears yet. Best for him to be full-grown before messing with senses of balance and hearing.

I pushed over to Jeffy. "What mods?" I demanded.

He was rubbing his ears curiously. "*I* don't know!"

"Show me," I said, pulling his hands away.

I bent his ear inside out and didn't see anything. But then a stray beam of light from one of the glitterfolk caught him, and gold wires shimmered like tiny lines of fire.

"What is it?" Jeffy demanded, squirming a bit.

"Hard to tell," I said. "It's so dark I can't really see." I stood, looking around at the milling glitterfolk. "Got a light, anyone?"

Several bodies flared with sudden blinding lights; not what I wanted or expected. Luckily, the mirror-man had a flashlight, which I accepted with thanks. I clicked it on to full power and examined Jeffy's ear again.

Gold wires gleamed. They trailed into the eardrum, though I couldn't tell how far. But I guessed, and my guess told me he had a lot of microwork inside there, all leading to a transmitter of some sort buried deep in his head. The gold wires were part of a broadcast antenna's mesh. They'd spread it through the fine hairs in his ear.

Hangman crowded in. After he had looked, he shook his head, fangs bared in anger.

"Well?" Jeffy asked.

"Hang on." I had one last check to run.

Digging out my new computer, I flicked it to Search mode and pressed it up against Jeffy's head. As I watched, it played through the frequencies and finally found the right one. Lights on its control panel blinked in rhythm to a loud, incessant beeping. Jeffy's ear was giving out quite a powerful little signal.

This time I had to give the dogs credit. Or the shadowcats. Whoever'd done it had effectively tagged Jeffy. And I never would have noticed, or thought to look: very slick, very professional. And very dangerous. I didn't like being outthought; that hit too close to home.

I looked at Hangman, but he shrugged helplessly. "Check us?"

Nerves jittering, I pressed the computer to his head; but nothing showed up. I let him do the same to me, and fortunately my scan was negative too. It made sense, in a way, their tagging only Jeffy. I wouldn't have left him behind for anything, and he certainly hadn't the experience to tell when his body had been tampered with.

Putting my computer away, I turned Jeffy's ear inside out again for a second look. He mewed uncomfortably.

"Be still," I told him. "This is important."

The more I examined the wiring, the more I knew I didn't want to mess with the transmitter. We'd need a real surgeon to get the deep parts out of him. The most I might do was disconnect the antenna, which would only dampen the signal, not kill it. And if they'd wired a detonator into him, set to explode if anything was tampered with . . . No, much better to see a professional.

Patting him on the shoulder, I let him straighten. Then I handed the flashlight back, thanked the glitterfolk, and watched them wander up the street. In seconds they vanished in the rolling smogbanks.

A burning landcar rolled silently past us, its only sounds the snap and crackle of melting plastics. I pulled back from the heat, shivering uneasily. From somewhere to the left, a rhythmic metal-on-metal pounding begin. *Lockup weather*.

Turning to Jeffy, slowly and honestly I told him what he had in his ear. I didn't sugar it down; he had a right to know what was going on.

When I finished, he gave a moan of despair. "What're we going to do?"

"Take you to ANIMEN-R-US," I said. "Grammatica can fix you up."

Hangman touched my shoulder. "They'll track us there."

I bit my lip. "We can't have him like this!"

"Don't betray your sources."

"So you want dogs following us?"

He shrugged again. He wouldn't meet my eye.

Jeffy looked from one of us to the other and back again. "What can we do?" he whispered.

Hangman settled back on his haunches. His stare told me: *You're the boss. You're his father*. You *think of something*.

I cursed and began to pace. *No-win any way you look. Damn them!* Drawing a deep breath, I choked, coughed, spat. *Got to get out of here*.

"It's my problem," Jeffy said. He took a step away. "You need someone to act as decoy, get them away from you while you work."

"What—" I began, puzzled.

"Sorry, Slash," he said. "See you soon's I can."

Then he turned and sprinted up the street. A marching line of glitterfolk appeared, shouting slogans:

"Tyranny and Villainy Triumph!"

"Seize the Best!"

"Generic's Junk!"

They parted ranks for an instant, and then he was gone. The darkness swallowed him.

"Crash the Parties!"

"Smash the Rich!"

I rose on two human feet. "Jeffy!" I called. "Get back here!"

Hangman caught my arm. "Let him go, Slash. It's best."

The glitterfolk paraded past, still shouting, and vanished into the smog. Suddenly I felt very, very alone.

"Jeffy!" I cried. Dropping to all fours, I sprinted into the smog after my kit.

Grayness surrounded me. I felt a blind, helpless rage building inside, at Jeffy for running away, at Rex and the dogs for bugging him, at Hatter and the shadowcats for betraying us. *Damn them all!*

The smog and dark had grown too thick; I could scarcely see. Every figure that loomed ahead of me turned out to be streeter or glitterfolk. More of them were flooding in from the alleys every minute, blocking traffic, distracting me. Once the smog thinned for a moment and I thought I glimpsed Jeffy far ahead, fleeing all out, and I called on all my reserves and ran as I had never run before. My heart thudded like a hammer in my chest; filthy air rasped in my lungs. Pavement flowed like water underfoot.

And then pain hit like a knife in the side. I skidded to a

halt, gasping for breath, clutching my stomach and trying not to be sick. Only then did it reach that I wasn't going to find him. I cursed my age, my shortcomings, my failures as both cat and father.

Jeffy, Jeffy. Gone, into the night.

If anything happened to him—

If anything happened to him, I'd find whoever had put that bug in his ear. I'd kill them if it took the rest of my life.

10

Hangman caught up with me not long after. I was just sitting there in the middle of the street watching the tidewaters of humanity flow past. My tail lashed. Because of the war stripes on my face, or perhaps (I thought) because I had a dangerous, nothing-left-to-lose gleam in my eye, passing streeters and glitterfolk alike left me strictly alone. *Desperate father. Do not provoke.*

Hangman as usual said nothing, just stood there beside me while I composed myself and caught my breath. Suddenly I wished I'd spent the money for a more versatile computer in the Tech-Tack-Toe; then I might have tracked Jeffy by his transmitter's signal. But I'd never needed to track anyone before. How could I have known I'd need to tonight?

Hindsight is a terrible thing.

I supposed, in time, we could have found something capable of following the transmitter's signal. But where would my kit be? I doubted the transmitter had a range of more than a few square blocks. No, Jeffy was gone. I just had to hope we'd really lost the dogs when the feet pulled their aircar down. Or that he would come to his senses and return.

All around us, glitterfolk danced, pranced, strutted their costumes. I saw the mirror-man and the skeleton and the bird lady again, all armed with axes, carrying between them what looked like a real wooden grandfather clock. Something broken inside chimed again and again and again. Overhead, lost in the gray of the smog, I heard the crunch of buckling metal, then cries of triumph that spread up and down the street, caught and carried like an echo.

I sucked a deep breath and looked at my old friend. "If they catch him—"

"He's not important."

"He is, because I *care* about him."

"Don't."

"How can you say that." I turned away, hurt. But I could see what he meant. If I didn't care, they couldn't use him against me. That would be best for him in the long run.

But how do you make yourself not care? How do you abandon your son?

"We'll find him later," Hangman said, and in a moment of rare compassion squeezed my shoulder. "Let's move."

We flowed through dark, smog-shrouded streets, two phantoms in the night. It didn't take long to reach the nearest transit station. There we caught a northbound platform, fleeing the lockup with thirty or forty others who looked grateful to be away.

I stood on the upper deck throughout the whole flight, staring down at the hazed-over lights of the city, letting the hurt and self-pity wash through me. How could I have let him go? Why hadn't I stopped him sooner? Why hadn't I insisted we take him to Grammatica—to *any* bodyshop?

I scarcely noticed when we landed at the Fishtown stop. The world had taken on unreal dimensions, everything muted, distant. Hangman had to call me, get me moving, and his voice sounded strangely hollow.

The usually short walk to Fishtown proper took forever. The streets seemed desolate tonight, as though all the warmth and friendliness cat territory usually exuded had been leeched away. Here and there catmen roamed the streets, playing and yowling through the night hours, but they seemed oddly different, like children playacting at being cats. I wondered for a time at my strange mood, then dismissed it as shock and worry. Clinical, yes; I could still be that. At least my mind still functioned on some level.

As we approached, a few catmen let out questioning cries, inviting us to join the sport. I ignored them. I couldn't play tonight, not with Jeffy out there alone.

It had been a long time since I hurt like this.

Hangman took a few unexpected turns, heading into the oldest part of cat territory. I'd hardly ever been here before: the houses were smaller and more run-down, the streets narrower, the atmosphere somehow dank and different from the pleasantly dim byways I normally associated with Fishtown. If Hangman spent his free time here, no wonder I'd never seen him at night.

Finally we stopped in front of a plain three-story house. A wreath decorated the door. Shades had been pulled in all the windows, but from the glow within more than token lights were burning: the residents were home.

"You're Peter Weston," he told me.

"Security?"

He nodded.

"Sure," I said.

"Do not tell my kits what we do. My wife knows, but everyone else thinks I sell insurance."

Wife? Kits? I gaped at him in surprise.

"I mean it, Slash." He padded smoothly up the steps and pressed his palm to the handpad. "Okay?"

"Whatever you want," I said.

The door gave a pleasant chirp of welcome and swung

open. Beyond, I had the impression of a large homey living room, full of cushions and children's toys.

He stood back to let me enter first. I padded forward into the brightness, blinking. From somewhere ahead came a low babble of voices. I glanced around; living room indeed, with well-worn scratching post in one corner and rolling, jingling, brightly colored toys scattered randomly across the floor.

"Home!" Hangman shouted as the door shut and relocked itself.

There was a moment of silence, then came delighted shrieks from the next room. Four young kits came hurtling in.

They all paused when they saw us standing there, him a father who'd left as a tiger and returned as something *black* with facial stripes, me a stranger looking much the same.

"Daddy?" the smallest one asked.

"Who else?" Hangman grinned, sat, and spread his arms.

That broke the dam. Shrieking again, they threw themselves on him, wrapping around chest, arms, neck.

"Careful—claws!" he cried, laughing.

"Daddy," said the tallest of the lot, stepping back. She was a girl, I thought. She couldn't have been more than six, and her calico skintights fit like a glove.

"What, Sally?"

She crouched as cat and leaped into his arms, snuggling up fiercely. I could hear her low, happy purring. "You were gone so long we thought dogs had eaten you!"

"There, there," he whispered soothingly. "No dog would even think of bothering me. It was just a long conference, that's all. Now I'm back. I'll be here for a while this time."

Another cat appeared in the doorway, this one an older and very much sexier calico. The kits' mother, I thought; Hangman's wife. She brushed against the doorway, tail high, purr throaty and loud. Her skintights had the same markings as little Sally's, I noted absently.

"Harry?" she asked. "What*ever* did you do to yourself?"

"Like it?"

"Tiger suits you better."

Hangman gave his children a final hug, disentangled himself, and went to her. They nuzzled briefly, then inclined their heads together. Their whispers came too low for me to catch. Probably settling my stay, I thought.

Meantime, I had fallen under the kits' scrutiny. From the way they stared, they might never have seen a catman before. I sat, wrapping tail around feet, and stared unblinkingly back at them.

As young kits went, these were cute enough, I supposed: slitted nightsight eyes (colored gold), plastic training claws, neatly groomed fur skintights (all calico save for the smallest, who had black panther), and tiny pointed ears—unscarred as yet from fights. The youngest, the panther, I took to be about three. The middle two looked about four, perhaps twins. Hangman had certainly wasted no time in starting them on the path to catdom.

It also made me realize how little I actually knew about Hangman. He'd always kept quiet regarding his personal life. But then, he'd kept quiet about most things. I never would have suspected this side of him existed: family cat, with mate and kits to feed and shelter. And he must have gone through quite a bit to distance himself from house and family. I ran security checks on him periodically—not to make sure of his loyalty, of course, but to make sure no information had crept into his files that I didn't want there. I ran similar checks on Jeffy and me every few months too, a simple routine precaution. But I'd never tagged onto this house, or any record of his marriage, or any record of his children. He must have set up an entirely different identity here. *Harry, she called him*. When I'd hired him, he'd told me his name was Sal Moretti, "but call me Hangman."

If he'd managed to keep all this a secret even from *me*, I

assumed it was safe here. Somehow, Hangman didn't strike me as the type to take chances with loved ones.

Which reminded me to be careful what I said around them: Hangman had said they didn't know anything about our dog-raiding business. And if his kits picked up even a hint of what we did, they might loose the information without re-alizing it.

"Who are you?" little Sally finally asked me.

"Pete," I told her. "I work with your father."

"Is he your boss?"

I smiled. "No. My partner."

Hangman led his wife over. "Kim, I'd like you to meet a friend of mine, Peter Weston. If it's okay with you, I'd like to put him up in the guest room. It'll just be for a couple of days."

"Of course," she said, giving me a cool smile. "Pleased to meet you, Peter. Have you eaten?"

"Well . . ." I looked at Hangman.

"There's always plenty," he said.

I felt like I'd come home.

After dinner, Hangman showed me to my room: a second-floor library that looked little used. Pillows against one wall would serve as bed. Shelves lined the other walls, all filled with real paper books: I'd never seen so many in one place before.

He must have noticed my surprise. "I collect them," he said proudly. "There are nearly two thousand here."

This was another facet to his personality I never would have suspected. Wife and children, and now paper books . . . I'd never realized there was so much to his life beyond the hatred toward dogs we both shared.

"How long have you been collecting them?" I asked.

"Since I was a kit." He took a slender volume from the shelf. It had been bound in real leather (I could smell it), and stamped in gold on the cover were the words "Favorite Poems of Emily Dickinson."

"Never heard of her," I said.

He nodded slowly. "When they put everything on-line, they left out so much—so many beautiful books. Today she's just a passing reference in a few of the academic databases, that's all. But once she was thought to be among the greatest American poets."

I shrugged uncomfortably. What did I know about books? About poetry? What did I care? Everything I needed was on-line. Facts, figures, information of any sort.

Hangman seemed to sense my opinion. He put the volume back without a word, but I could tell he was disappointed. Pulling an extra blanket from the trunk under the shaded window, he tossed it to me.

"Tomorrow," he said, "we find Jeffy."

As I lay abed, my thoughts turned once again to Hangman's wife and kits. They all seemed so happy, so ordinary, as though Hangman really were the insurance salesman he claimed. *This is what my life should have been like*, I thought. *Normal, ordinary, married to my wonderful wife, raising my wonderful children with her.*

I shuddered, and felt a pang of loss so sharp I thought my heart would burst. *Dear Jamie, how long has it been since you died?*

Sometimes I could still hear her if I listened, still feel her lying beside me at night. If I reached out, I would be able to touch her.

I rolled over. A pale blue-gray glow filtered in through the window's shade, but it showed the emptiness better than a floodlight. *Alone.*

I'd never been so alone as that first night after she'd died. *Murdered by dogs.* That's why I hunted them. That's why I killed them, stole what they valued. Because they'd stolen Jamie from me.

I pressed my eyes shut, and every detail flooded back with a crystalline clarity.

It had been one of those long, hot summer days, with tar melting on the roads and sidewalks so hot you could fry eggs on them. The cloudless blue sky, the sun a dazzling white-gold . . .

I sat sweating in my office over mortgage reports. The 'freshers had broken down, the repairmen hadn't arrived yet, and the Redstone file had to be in my boss's computer to-morrow morning. He'd scheduled an important meeting with one of the senior vice presidents and needed all the numbers crunched, lined up, and made to do the proper tricks, *just so*.

I called up the file again. I'd just processed the figures for the third time, and they still didn't work.

I remembered all that. Every event of that whole day seemed indelibly etched into my memory; I'd relived it in dream and nightmare so often, I couldn't have forgotten if I'd tried.

The vidphone rang, and when I tabbed it on, I found myself looking at a very old, very tired, very sad man in a black uniform. He showed me his badge, introducing himself as Captain Reed, then said, "Mr. Carter, I'm afraid I have some bad news for you."

Panic swelled. "What—"

"It's your wife, sir." And I listened in stunned silence as he told me about the terrorist attack on the turbostation. How Jamie had been one of several people caught in the bomb's blast. How sorry he was for my loss. How they'd only been able to identify her from her purse, but could I please come down and look at her, to make sure?

"What about my children?" I asked numbly.

"Can you describe them, please?"

"Twins. A boy and a girl, both seven—"

"I think you better come down here, sir," he said softly. "I'll send a car."

"That will take too long. I'll catch a taxi." Feeling wooden, I switched off the phone.

Time blurred. I seemed to be walking in a dream. I recall getting a cab down to the turbostation, walking up to a cordoned-off area surrounded by gaping crowds. Captain Reed was there. He escorted me through police lines.

An entire bank of storage lockers had been hit by the bomb's blast; plastic and metal alike had torn and melted. In front of lockers I saw scattered puddles of blood, and what looked like a severed hand. As I watched, a uniformed woman picked up the hand with tongs and sealed it into a container. Then she calmly and methodically tagged and labeled it.

"Here," Reed said, not unkindly, taking my elbow and guiding me toward a series of sheet-covered bodies. More red puddled the floor here. Shrapnel from the lockers must have cut people pretty badly, I realized.

He moved down the row of bodies, stopped, pulled back one sheet. There she lay, Jamie sure enough, her face pale from loss of blood, her eyes closed. She almost seemed asleep. I reached out to touch her, but Reed pulled my hand back.

"It's better if you don't."

"My children?"

"Here." He pulled back another sheet, turning his head away. His voice broke. "I'm sorry. I'm so sorry."

Little Carl didn't have much of a face anymore, but I recognized his clothes, his hair. And Debra lay beside him, as serene in death as she'd ever been in life.

I couldn't look either. It made me sick.

In a weak voice, I demanded, "Who did it?"

"Anarchist dogmen. They'd been threatening it for months, but nobody believed them . . ."

"Dogs," I said.

Turning, I looked back at Jamie. Reed had covered her up again. Only not with a sheet now, with something else. Was it . . . a flag?

I blinked. Two images seemed to be superimposing on each other. Both were very similar, yes, both death scenes, I thought.

In the first, I clearly saw Jamie as I remembered her, lying in that turbostation covered by a sheet. Feet milled about in the background, jotting things down in notebooks, taking holos, or just talking and sipping cups of coffee.

But at the same time I also saw a roped-off street, a funeral cart being drawn by four black horses, with thousands of pale flowers massed around a flag-shrouded coffin. An American flag, red and blue and white, with all sixty stars in place.

I concentrated on the street, on the flag. All of a sudden it came clear, like a picture suddenly snapping into focus, and I was *there*. Like at the dogs' attack on my house, literally *there* in every sense of the word. I felt the bright sun on my face, smelled the sweet scent of lilac on the breeze, heard the murmur of crowds, heard horses' hooves plodding dully on pavement. And farther up the street I now saw a series of such funeral carts, perhaps as many as twenty.

What, I wondered, *the bloody hell* is *this*?

11

It has to be the PED, I realized, amazed. There are old
memories stored on it. I hadn't even considered the possibility.

My viewpoint swung suddenly, and I found myself looking
at two people, the first a man of perhaps thirty-five or forty,
with a narrow, pinched face, sharp Roman nose, and close-
cropped black hair. He had the pale skin of a man who seldom
ventured out in daylight.

The second was a thin, almost emaciated woman. She wore
her reddish-brown hair long on the sides and short in front.
She had a hard, intense expression, and I took an instant
dislike to her. Had anyone asked, I couldn't have defined
why precisely; her face just hit all the wrong notes. Cruel
lips, cold eyes, the look of a killer, I thought. A pistol tucked
casually into her belt cemented that impression. I wondered
what she needed a pistol for.

The pinch-faced man licked his lips and said something
nervously. I didn't understand the language, but I identified
it readily enough as French.

The woman barked, "*Non!*" Her voice held a sneer.

"Speak English," I felt myself say. "I don't like it when I can't understand you."

"You've done your job, Robert," the woman said to me in flawless American-accented English. "Relax. We'll get you the hell out of here soon enough." She pulled a stimtab from her pocket and flicked it to light with her thumb, sucking hungrily. I caught a faint whiff of its sweet, soothing drugsmoke.

I glanced at the pinch-faced man. When he nodded curtly, I returned to the window and gazed down into the street again. Horses had carried the first funeral cart below my window. A grainy hologram flickered above and behind the casket, I noticed: a man's head projected life-size. He'd been middleaged when the holo was taken, and in this shot he smiled faintly, as though he'd just been let in on some grand joke. Probably taken from a little holocube, I thought, the kind his wife would keep on her desk at work. They'd enlarged it for the funeral, which explained its soft focus.

The dead man had to be American because of the flag, and someone important to warrant crowds like these. I glanced up the street at the other carts. Several of those bore American flags, too, but most of the rest seemed to be French. Thousands, perhaps tens of thousands, had turned out to see this death parade. Some men wore black armbands; some women wore black veils. A number cried openly.

I concentrated on the holoed face behind the first casket. Something struck me familiar about it, though I didn't know quite what. Then it all snapped into place.

He was Underhill. *The* Underhill: James Patrick Underhill IV, United States senator, assassinated in Paris several weeks ago in some sort of bombing. It made headlines for days. Some terrorist organization, I didn't remember which one, had claimed responsibility. Hadn't there been something else, too? It seemed to me they'd caught the assassins—

Someone rapped twice on the door, then twice again. I

jumped, startled, and looked back. One hand dropped to the gun at my belt.

The red-haired woman crossed to the door, asked something in French, and received a terse reply.

"Who's that?" I demanded.

"Jean-Claude," the thin-faced man replied. "Your driver."

"Oh." I relaxed; someone expected, someone safe.

The door swung open. The man outside held a pistol too, and he pointed it at me as he entered.

I stepped back. "Hey!"

"Don't worry," the woman said to me. She suddenly had her pistol out too, as did the pinch-faced man. "It won't hurt long," she said. "It's just too wild now to get you out now. They're going door-to-door looking for you, and they have a sketch. So I'm afraid Jacques and I are back to normal business. We tracked you here and burst into your room, surprising you. You had a gun and we shot in self-defense. Sorry, Robert. Nothing personal."

I grabbed for the pistol at my belt, but I never had a chance. The three of them fired point-blank. It seemed impossible, so much like a bad vid. But their pistols really did roar, and fire really did flash from the barrels. I heard it, saw it.

Then the room swung crazily. I found myself lying on the floor, staring up at them through a red haze. I smelled burnt gunpowder, sharp and unpleasant, and darkness seemed to be creeping in around the edges of my vision, the start of an endless spiral into oblivion.

But I hadn't felt the impact of the bullets. In fact, I didn't feel a thing.

"Terrorists," the red-haired woman said, shaking her head. I focused on her hard, cruel face. She laughed, and it felt as if winter had come.

Everything faded like a dam had burst, and darkness instead of water poured through.

"Callisto," I heard myself whisper.

Then—

The memory just ended.

Shuddering, I sat up, stunned. I'd just experienced death, I realized with a sort of disbelieving horror. They'd killed the PED-me. Shot him in that room. I hadn't felt the last rattle of breath in Robert's throat. But it was close enough. *Too* close.

"Callisto" must have been his memory-save phrase, just as "black rabbit" was mine. I hoped Robert (whoever he was, wherever he was) would rest better knowing someone had discovered his murder, his betrayal.

And I now had the feeling I'd stumbled onto a major piece of the puzzle, perhaps the key I needed to unlock the truth. Dogs, shadowcats, I realized they hadn't been after the machinery of the PED. They'd wanted the memories stored on its disk. And if this was any indication of information I now carried, I didn't blame them. *Assassinations. Murders. Bombings.* Very messy business indeed.

Several questions loomed. Why had dogs been smuggling Robert's severed head into the country? Who were Jacques, Jean-Claude, and the red-haired woman working for? Why had they killed Robert? And what were they doing at Senator Underhill's funeral parade?

I frowned. No easy answers occurred to me. I needed more data.

Were there other memories stored on my PED? I'd stumbled onto Robert's murder by accident, triggering recall with a similar memory. If I went *seeking* foreign memories . . .

Closing my eyes, I leaned back. *There's only one way to find out.*

Concentrating on Senator Underhill, thinking about Paris and assassinations—

Images began to form. *Got it.*

* * *

My field of vision consisted of a small room with a single window. I sat on a king-size bed assembling a weapon of some kind. All the pieces had been clipped inside a large leather case, and I pulled them out and snicked them into position with an experienced hand. I'd done this before, from the look of things; I even wore tight rubber gloves to keep from leaving fingerprints behind.

Snapping barrel and stock into place, I found myself holding a massive laser-sighted rifle of some kind. I'd never seen one this large before. And when I pulled out its fist-size projectile, it looked more like a miniature missile than a bullet. I fitted the shell into place, clicked the hammer back, and nodded happily. Raising the rifle, I squinted through the scope. A red grid overlaid my field of vision. Numbers filled the left-hand side; strange symbols filled the right.

"Ready," I said, putting it down.

"Good."

I turned and found the red-haired woman who'd murdered me standing by the window. She parted the curtains, looking out.

Joining her, I gazed through an open window onto a wide avenue below. Landcars snaked past, caught in a traffic jam, and I wondered that so many were in use here: definitely not America.

We were perhaps eight or nine floors up. A towering office complex, walls done in mirrored glass, stood directly across from us. We might have been in any city, I thought; all places tended to look much the same these days, a creeping uniformity for the Global Village set. Only to the right, in the distance, I noticed the Eiffel Tower. It looked smaller than I'd thought it would, somehow—not the great monument to human engineering shown on vids or picture cards, but more of a huge metal sculpture, fenced in by a ring of taller buildings.

So indeed this had to be Paris, where Senator Underhill had been assassinated. And I had a strange feeling about what came next.

"You got the plan straight?" the red-haired woman asked.

"Yeah," I said.

"Then I'll leave you to it."

She dropped the curtain and strode to the door. Opening it a crack, she peeped through, waited for someone to pass, then left. The door hissed shut automatically behind her.

I waited till the lock clicked, then pulled back the curtain and stood impatiently watching the street. I had a sinking feeling inside.

Finally, several minutes later, a large black limousine hovered into view. Everything about it screamed power and money, from the bristle of microwave relay dishes on its roof to the extra-lift repellers mounted underneath. From the way it handled, it had to be several tons overweight . . . armored, I thought.

As it settled in front of the office building, I flew to work. I pulled up a chair, sat straddling its back, and rested the rifle's barrel on the windowsill. Using the target-finder to zero in on the aircar's door, I gently touched the trigger, waiting.

The first four men to climb from the limo were all dressed in gray suits and dark sunglasses. Bulges under their left shoulders marked guns: hired muscle, I decided. They stood looking about cautiously.

Meantime, a group of men and women hurried down from the office building. They looked important: silk suits, expensive ties, real leather shoes. Probably the powermakers of France come to meet and greet Underhill.

As they neared, a tall, heavyset man eased from the limo. He wore a dark blue suit with a pale pink tie, and diamond rings glinted on his fingers. Through the viewscope I saw his face, smiling, jovial, close enough that I might have been standing next to him: Senator Underhill. I recognized him instantly.

That jittery feeling inside me grew worse. I tried to shout, to warn Underhill, but I couldn't make a sound. I tried to stop myself from taking aim, though I knew deep inside it could never work, that all this had already taken place weeks before, that events would carry me inexorably forward as an unwilling observer.

I nudged something on the target-finder. Numbers flashed on the scope's grid; a red light touched Underhill's forehead for a split second.

Then I squeezed the rifle's trigger. I ached from trying to stop myself.

Underhill's head splattered like a melon hit with a baseball bat. An instant later, a harsh white light flared, brighter than the sun, brighter than any light I'd ever seen before.

I ducked down, rubbing my eyes. The floor shook faintly, and I heard a distant rumble, like an avalanche growing closer. Slowly it faded.

I didn't wait to see more. Crossing to the center of the room, I tossed my rifle onto the bed beside its case, folded the sheet to cover both, and walked quickly to the door. Outside, as I waited for the elevator, I pulled off my gloves and stuffed them into my pocket.

When the elevator came, I punched the ground-floor button with one knuckle and rode silently to street level. My every motion had a calm, businesslike precision. *Job well done*, I thought bitterly. I hated Robert intensely at that moment.

Outside, all traffic had come to a stop. Several aircars burned; people sat stunned, or wandered through the crowds with blank looks on their faces. The breeze carried smells of burnt plastic, rubber, flesh. Distantly, I heard a woman screaming. Farther off, sirens wailed—help coming too late. Underhill and everyone around him had died instantly.

I began to whistle as I turned and headed up the street without a backward glance. "Callisto," I said suddenly.

And that memory was over too.

I searched for more memories after that, but didn't find any. Either Robert hadn't saved others, or I didn't have the right mental key to unlock them. Even so, Underhill's assassination was enough to haunt my sleep for weeks to come.

Lying there, images of death flickering through my every thought, I spent one of the worst nights of my life. I saw Underhill's head explode again and again, the shot echoing in my mind. I saw the flash of light, the burning aircars, all the death and chaos. And over it all loomed the red-haired woman, puppetmaster, puller of strings, far worse than Robert ever could have been. I had the distinct impression she'd ordered the assassination. And that, if she knew anything about me, about what I had and what I'd seen, she'd order my assassination too. She was a terrorist, brutal as they came, with no qualms or conscience about what she did. Just like the anarchist dogmen who had killed my Jamie so long ago.

Shivering, soaked with sweat, I untabbed my skintights at the throat and took deep, cleansing breaths, trying to relax, trying to make myself believe I'd get out of it all alive. Now it all seemed so hopeless.

Those memories. No wonder so many people had been trying to kill me, trap me, blackmail me. I'd seen the true powers behind Underhill's assassination, the red-haired woman and Jacques and Jean-Claude.

The terrorists needed to protect themselves.

The government wanted to capture Underwood's killers.

And they were all after me.

And yet . . .

And yet the more I thought about it, the more things still didn't quite make sense. If our government wanted to catch

Underhill's killers, why not simply ask for the PEDs back? Why make such a big fuss about it? Why not explain the circumstances and appeal to my patriotism, at least as a first try? I would have started that way if *I* were them. For a matter of national security, to avenge Senator Underhill, of *course* I would have cooperated. I had no love of fearmongers; I'd suffered my own loss to them. I *knew* what it felt like. For Underhill, I would have turned in my PED (or at least its data disk) without a moment's hesitation.

Then I mentally slapped myself. *Stupid*. My PED had belonged to an assassin. I'd watched everything through *his* eyes.

What would a common assassin be doing with a PED?

I took a step back and began a new line of reasoning. Granted, PEDs had been developed in China. Most of the world's entertainment industry centered there; where else would they push research into event-recording and playback?

Granted, the Chinese government had taken over development of the PEDs. PEDs made great tools for spies; any soldier worth his pay would have realized that. Considering how close President Xu's regime kept its ties to the United States, and considering how often Chinese and U.S. agencies worked together, I thought it safe to assume the Chinese had shared their PED-research information with us. What better way to cement an alliance than sharing secrets?

And our government's labs had perfected the PEDs without telling the Chinese. Sneaky, yes, but expectedly so. That's why Pietr thought there shouldn't be working models: his source of information said the Chinese government didn't have them perfected yet. *But we did*.

The cumulative weight of evidence seemed irrefutable. Robert, the assassin, my PED's first owner, must have been an American working for our government. Which meant our government had murdered Senator Underhill.

Suddenly, the whys didn't matter all that much; enough that my own government had killed a senator. Perhaps Underhill had stepped over political boundaries and trod on the wrong toes. Perhaps he'd threatened the wrong people. Or perhaps his policies had been too idiosyncratic, too idealized, and the higher powers decided his son would prove a more tractable senator after he inherited. None of that seemed important to me. I felt raw anger and disgust, and knew I as an American had been betrayed.

It now seemed a silly childlike sort of innocence, but I'd believed in my government. Everyone said ours was the greatest country to rise since ancient Rome, and the incorruptible good intentions of our government had been one of the things I'd taken for granted, alongside the love of family, the trust of friends, and the stupidity of dogs.

So I'd always paid my taxes, always cooperated with the government whenever possible. I never complained when they lost forms or misplaced files I uploaded to their computers. I did my part, and in return they gave me security, maintaining national and international stability, keeping up the roads and sidewalks, the computer bases, the welfare programs. The government worked for the good of all. And, if I ever got into trouble, I knew I could always call on them for help. That's what feet were for, right?

But to have the government take so much authority on itself, to have it making life-and-death decisions regarding people like Senator Underhill and me . . . no, that was certainly wrong.

Then it occurred to me that the government as a whole would never be able to act with such ruthless decision. Rather, some small branch had to be responsible. It all had to narrow down to one person, or group of people, with a lot of power. The whole government hadn't suddenly gone bad, just one part, like a single rotten apple in a huge basket.

* * *

Dawn had come. I rose and stretched, joints creaking. No sense trying to sleep with the sun up, I thought, especially not after all these world-shaking revelations.

Deeply unhappy, I padded down to the kitchen. Fluorescents glowed; the vid burbled a cheery news program. Hangman lay atop heaped pillows, lapping coffee.

"Want some?" he asked, and when I nodded he rose and poured me a bowl too.

Sometime during the night he'd recolored his face gray, covering the Indian war-paint stripes. He looked a lot better without them. He'd also changed into gray panther skintights, which suited him nearly as well as tiger, and in fact added a quiet sort of dignity to his appearance. The major cats—tigers, lions—had always struck me as too ostentatious. They were flashy, likely to attract attention among humans because they *did* stand out. I'd only tolerated Hangman's tigerform because he had the talent and personality to go with it.

I listened for a moment, but didn't hear anything except the ticking of an antique clock from the living room. "Where's your family?" I asked.

"Sleeping."

"Good," I said. "We need to talk." And as we drank, I filled him in on everything I'd found that night, including my line of reasoning that brought me to accuse our government of murder.

His tail twitched at various points in the story, but he remained silent throughout. Only when I'd finished did he show any emotion: he gave a long, low sigh.

"Underhill," he said slowly, "wanted to disband SecurNet."

That pricked my ears. "How's that?"

"His big push. Government didn't need thugs and bullies, more military and feet would do better."

I nodded to myself. SecurNet certainly had the means to murder Underhill while he was on a goodwill tour of France. And, with their emphasis on national security, they would be politically aware enough to blame it all on anti-American terrorists, of which the world seemed quite full of late. It made me wonder, then, how many jet crashes, how many bombings, how many more murders did they arrange each year in the name of freedom?

I shook my head. We still didn't know one way or another that SecurNet had arranged *any*thing. To act, we'd need proof. Or at least more than mere conjecture, and certainly more than what was on the PED.

I told Hangman as much. "Perhaps," I added slowly, "it's time we started using the PED ourselves."

"How?"

"Information. It seems key to everything here."

"The red coupes," he said suddenly. "Look at them again."

"Easy to do," I said. *Perhaps we missed something there.*

I leaned back, closing my eyes, and thought of the attack on my house. It could have been a year ago, as far as I was concerned, so much had happened since.

It all came back sharp as life. Landing on the roof, yes, and finding the warning lights in the lift. Retreating to the aircar, taking off.

I slowed the flow of images as little red coupes rose around us. And there I found the answer, staring me in the face where it had been all along: registration marks on the aircars. I'd been too busy running at the time to notice, but the PED had caught them all.

"Take this down," I said, and froze the image before me. It blurred a bit, more a grainy 2-D photograph rather than a live experience, but I could still read everything.

"Go," Hangman said, voice distant, barely reaching me.

I reeled off registration marks of the three coupes in view. Then I let the ambush progress and got two more. That was surely enough for our purposes.

I opened my eyes and found Hangman staring intently at me, pocket computer in hand, information keyed in.

"That's it," I said. "Now it's just a matter of tracking down the owners."

He stood and put his bowl in the sink. "I'll find out," he said. Tucking his pocket computer away, he headed for the door.

When I followed, he shook his head. "Too many people looking for you."

"But—"

"Not like that in daylight. I'll bring you better dye and new skintights."

"Okay." I sat, tail around my feet, whiskers trembling with impatience. "You're sure you can find out who owns the coupes?"

He nodded once.

Hangman's wife rose not long after that. She made large breakfasts for me and her children, then ushered them off to school; it seemed they were in some accelerated learning program and couldn't afford to be even a few minutes late. After that, she had to go to work—she sold real estate and specialized in Fishtown properties, she said—and wouldn't be back till suppertime.

Hangman returned half an hour after they left, face unreadable as ever, a package under his arm. He tossed it to me, and through the wrapping I saw tan fur. Cougar skintights; not my favorite, but they would do. I had more important things to worry about than how I looked.

"And?" I said impatiently. "Who owns the coupes?"

"SecurNet."

Somehow, I wasn't surprised.

12

Hangman dyed my face. He'd bought several different bottles of coloring, all browns ranging in shade from almost-blacks to almost-whites, and he mixed them over the sink, applying first one treatment to my whole face, then another to just my cheeks, then a third to just my ears. He did touch-up with cotton balls, then stood back and grunted approval.

I looked in a mirror. He'd done a truly fine job, completely hiding the stripes, then matting and recoloring the glitterpaint to a more natural sandy-brown color. He'd left my ears a bit darker, and given me a faint trace of liver-spotting about the whiskers. Perfection.

In my room, I changed into the cougar skintights Hangman had brought. They fit like a glove. When I dropped to catform and padded back in forth before the wall mirror, admiring my sharp new looks, I felt like a kit getting his first catmods. Nobody would recognize me now, I thought, not even Jeffy . . . which was exactly how I wanted it. I hated being easily tagged; far better to move freely.

If only Jeffy were here, I'd feel like celebrating. Safe in

Fishtown, well disguised, finally getting on top of the PED and the plots around us . . . our prospects were looking up for the first time since we'd ambushed those smugglers.

Poor Jeffy. I hated thinking of him out there. Was he lost and wandering the streets, afraid to take shelter lest dogs find him? Or had he been picked up, ruthlessly questioned by SecurNet? The more I wondered, the more worried I became. At least, I thought, I'd trained him as best I could for the real world. Given half a chance, he'd make out okay. I had to trust him to come out on top.

Only—who had planted the transmitter in his ear, Rex or the shadowcats? I had a feeling it would make a difference in his chances. Dogs didn't feel any compunctions against harming catmen. And there had been two different packs of dogs after us, I reminded myself. If SecurNet got him . . . I didn't want to think about it. I knew from the PED how easily SecurNet killed.

The whole idea of dogs working for SecurNet disturbed my sense of propriety. People went dog—and cat, and bird, and all other animalforms—because of dissatisfaction with humanity. You didn't pay to have yourself reconstructed as an animal unless you were pretty desperate. You had to sever your ties with true men, move beyond them to a better life. You couldn't by definition *be* a proper animan if you kept a regular job with humans. You had to part with your human side and live and work and play as though you truly were the animal you'd become. To be an animalform human working for SecurNet . . .

The smugglers were dogs, too, I recalled uneasily. *And how many dogs in those red coupes—twenty? thirty?*

If SecurNet had so many dogmen working for them, dogkind hadn't just been infiltrated, it had been completely subverted. Or perhaps Rex had sold out the rest of animalkind for special favors from SecurNet. I frowned. That last might be the real answer. Dogmen had done some pretty odd things in the past, like trying to form their own sports teams for competition with humans.[1] Perhaps switching loyalties to our parent race was their latest move.

Then why didn't Rex turn us over to SecurNet when he had us?

I found it all very confusing.

At least catkind was safe from SecurNet. We were too proud, too aloof from mainline humanity, to ever go back. The moment I'd gone cat, I'd found myself in a very protective, very insular society. An unwritten law said cats were better than humans (and better than dogs, and all other animen for that matter). It served to reinforce our decisions to *be* cats . . . self-protection for our fragile little society and our fragile little egos. I'd embraced the cats-are-better belief *because* it bound us together. I knew dogs, despite their stupidities, would have a protective worldview too, an us-against-the-rest philosophy to make them a single people rather than a ragtag collection of self-mutilating freaks.

Or perhaps the dogs' reasons for cooperating with SecurNet were completely different. Who knew how dogs thought? It would come clear in the end, I thought. For now, I'd have to wait and see.

"And," Hangman said, when I returned to the kitchen, "I know where the coupes are kept."

I focused on him. "How did you find out?"

He seemed quite happy with himself. "I asked vehicle registration."

I doubted it was that easy. "What did you tell them?"

---

[1] Most sports commissions immediately ruled dog-teams illegal because all their athletes had synthetics-enhanced bodies. The one sporting event that permitted dogmen to compete was the new trans-Alaska dogsled race. David Norton (full human) ran a team of eight dogmen through the ten-day cross-country course, finishing eighth out of nine competitors. (The ninth withdrew on the second day of the race when her lead dog [full canine] broke his leg.)

"They dropped a package and I wanted to return it."

"Great!" I said. How willingly people believed in good deeds, even this day, even in the Sprawl. "Let's go have a look. And maybe while we're out, we can find Jeffy."

"Sure," he said. But he didn't seem that confident about finding my kit.

Hangman wrote his wife a quick note saying we'd be back for dinner, then we trooped up to the roof. Canvas shrouded something at the far end, and that's where we headed. He paused before it for a second, glanced at me, and then slowly, ceremoniously, reached out and whisked it off.

Beneath the canvas sat a two-seater aircar, low and sleek as they came: a classic Jaguar 44, the best they made. You couldn't see through its dark, tinted windows, and its black paint shone like polished onyx.

"Nice," I said, approving. I wondered how he'd been able to afford it and children too on what we made. "Not exactly unobtrusive, though."

"It is where we're going."

He ran his hand down the Jag's front windshield as though caressing a lover, then touched the pad on the driver's side. Its computer verified his prints instantly. Both doors popped open.

We slid into plush seats. A rubbery, new-car smell lingered inside. Hangman hadn't driven it much, I thought, and I didn't blame him. Why risk an accident? Owning a car like this was like owning a work of art.

My seat adjusted itself, asking if I felt comfortable. It thanked me politely when I said I did.

Hangman clicked the ignition cube into place. Control readouts sprang to life, and he started through a full power-up check. I noted, from the readout, that he hadn't driven the car in nearly four months; that's why he was verifying everything.

At last the checks proved out. When he pushed the cube a notch farther, the Jag started instantly, powerful repeller fields purring to life.

We lifted fast. Hangman banked through a turn, then headed centerSprawl at a good clip. As soon as we merged with southbound traffic, he switched on the autopilot and let it cruise.

I watched buildings flowing past and pondered the mysterious ways of dogs and SecurNet. Nothing new occurred to me, no great plans to put them off our trail or find Jeffy, no great revelations which knocked everything into place.

At one point I told Hangman about my concerns over dogkind selling out, and he didn't seem as dubious as I was. He could, he said, see dogs doing quite a few things—working for SecurNet among them.

Forty minutes into our trip, the autopilot beeped. Hangman took control and dropped us into slower traffic, circling down. I leaned forward expectantly.

"That's it," he said.

I followed his finger to a building so huge it took up an entire city block. Ninety stories high, mirrored glass walls, rooftop parking lot—your typical office complex grown out of control.

It came up fast below us, and he slowed, taking a good long look. A steady stream of people poured through front and side doors; aircars landed and left the roof every few seconds. The place bustled like an ant colony.

I scanned the aircars. At the far end of the parking lot, clustered together, I saw perhaps forty red coupes like the ones the dogs had used.

"There they are!" I said.

Hangman spotted them too, and let out a triumphant snort. Then, instead of moving on, instead of finding a safe vantage point on another building from which to watch, he circled us down.

"Are you crazy?" I demanded, twisting in my seat. "They'll catch us, cert!"

"Unlikely."

He toggled the landing lights and put down on SecurNet's building. His Jaguar fit neatly between two other sporty aircars, perhaps thirty meters from the red coupes. We could see them perfectly. He shut off all lights, and there we sat, helpless.

At least, I thought, we were safely hidden behind darkened windows. Little help. I moaned inwardly, expecting someone to charge over and demand to know who we were and what we were doing on government property. I pressed my face to the window and looked as far to each side as I could see.

"Relax," he said. "Nobody will bother."

"You can't be sure about that." Suddenly I pointed toward the nearest series of lifts. Three men in gray one-piece daysuits were already headed for us.

Hangman said nothing. He just sat while I fidgeted, ignoring me. And when those men got into an old sedan two aircars down, he let out an explosive laugh.

It was going to be a long day, I could tell.

Nobody touched the coupes as morning crept past and afternoon edged toward evening. I'd begun to think the coupes were used only for specific missions, that we wouldn't see anybody leave in one. Eyes slitted, I half dozed, watching people as they entered my line of sight.

Suddenly a woman walked past. I jerked upright, all sorts of alarms jangling inside.

She was thin, almost emaciated, with sharp features and short reddish-brown hair. Her black one-piece suit pulled tight at throat and wrists; gold buttons flashed in the sun. A briefcase swung at her side.

I knew her instantly, from her face down to her economical walk. She'd murdered Robert. She'd supervised Senator Underhill's assassination. She was the woman from Paris, the woman from my PED memories.

Quickly I told Hangman. He began powering up his Jag.

The red-haired woman climbed into one of the red coupes and lifted without a moment's hesitation. She headed due west. Rich people lived out there, I knew, on vast estates or in exclusive condo complexes. It verified my suspicions that she was more than a mere SecurNet underling. She had to be high up to afford all that.

We followed. Hangman kept well back, so far that at times I thought we'd lost her, but then he'd nose forward and I'd just pick out her coupe out against the stream of other aircars headed home for the day. My excitement built. I let claws ripple from my fingertips and bared my fangs. It felt good to be the hunter instead of the hunted.

Finally she nosed down toward a sprawlingly vast ten-story building. Lush green lawns surrounded it. Beyond lay an Olympic-size swimming pool, tennis courts, jogging track, and all the other exercise areas a person could ever want. Oh, yes, she was living the good life on our taxes.

She pulled into an underground parking garage. Thirty seconds later, we followed.

A guard sat in a little booth, watching aircars come and go, but he barely glanced at Hangman's Jaguar 44. The gate was raised; we entered. Of course he'd let us through, I thought. Anyone owning a Jag had to be rich enough to live here.

The red-haired woman had her own parking space, of course. We followed her down a level, then pulled in five spaces beyond her, putting a white limousine between us. Hangman powered down.

When I popped the door, Hangman grabbed my arm.

"She'll be armed," he whispered. He opened the glove compartment. Inside, clipped in place, lay a small energy pistol. I recognized it; state-of-the-art, enough power in its battery to burn a fist-sized hole through any human in half a second.

I took it, and we climbed out. The red-haired woman was just starting for the lift twenty meters away.

Padding forward, silent as two ghosts, we closed. She didn't hear us till the last moment, and when she turned, puzzled, she didn't have a chance—Hangman had already pounced.

He caught her shoulders, driving her to the concrete floor. She rolled, and he rolled with her, coming up on top, pinning her. When she tried to heave him off, he crushed her wrists in his hands until she gasped in pain. Then, resigned, she lay back, eyes boiling hate.

I held the energy pistol ready in case she tried anything more. But it didn't come to that. She took it very coolly when he searched her. From her belt he pulled an energy pistol smaller than mine. Her boots hid a pair of thin throwing knives. A gold bracelet held a coil of thin wire, perfect for strangling. Aside from keys and briefcase (both of which I appropriated), she now had nothing but her clothes.

Hangman stood, satisfied, covering her with her own energy pistol. I motioned her to her feet.

"Hatter is meat," she said tightly. "How *dare* you—"

"Shut up," I said. "Back to your coupe. *Move!*"

It took several minutes to go through her briefcase. She leaned against her coupe all the while, Hangman covering her. I scanned files and opened pouches as fast as I could, discovering several sets of ID cards: one in French for a Marie Patrice, one in German for a Hilda Werner, and one in English for a SecurNet supervisor named Jan Harris. All three carried her picture.

"Now we're getting somewhere," I said. "Jan Harris . . . Marie Patrice . . . Hilda Werner . . ." None of them rang any bells, and none brought up more PED memories.

She looked puzzled. "You're not from Hatter, are you?" she finally asked.

"Now you're catching on."

"Then who?"

I didn't bother to answer. I pulled a packet from her brief-case and flicked it open. Inside were folders with various names I recognized—mine, Jeffy's, and Hangman's among them. Also Pietr Von Klausch (his marked "canceled"), Esteban Grammatica, and Paul Williamson—Grammatica's dog-assistant. Several more (all marked "canceled") had names I didn't recognize, but when I opened them I saw pictures of the dogmen we'd killed to steal the PEDs. *Canceled* . . . doubtless a SecurNet euphemism for dead. Which meant they'd murdered Pietr, but not Jeffy as yet.

"Ah," I said. "Perfect." *Lots of reading tonight.*

I tucked the folders back into her briefcase. I'd found what I wanted, all right. Now I'd know how much they had on us.

"Well?" Hangman asked. "Drug her?"

"Don't bother," she said. "I'm psychoscreened. You should know that, if—" Her eyes narrowed. She looked at me more carefully. "Slash?" she asked.

"Very good," I said, smiling. Then to Hangman I said, "Kill her."

"Slash," she said softly, "you're making a mistake. You're interfering in things you have no business with. It's not too late—we can still work things out."

"How?"

"Give me the one remaining PED. No harm done, right? You're after money—I'll pay. Very generously."

"One remaining PED?"

"I already have the one you sold Von Klausch."

"How?"

"You don't want to know."

I swallowed uneasily.

She went on. "Give it to me and I'll call off the investigation."

"It can't be that simple."

"Of course it is. We're bureaucracy; things get lost. And when it's just paper in a secret filing system—shred a few documents and they're gone. Forever."

"No more problems with dogs?"

"That's right. You just retire. Perhaps we can set you up in your own business, something to keep you busy, away from dogs and smugglers. We've done that before."

I laughed. "All that concern for me. How kind!" My face grew hard. "I know all about Paris, how you killed Robert and Senator Underhill. You SecurNet murderers aren't going to get away with it!"

She sighed. "No matter how it seems, we really *are* working for the good of the country. SecurNet deals with events on a global scale. With the future of America as a whole. Individuals don't matter—it's their cumulative effect."

"You've lost me," I said.

"Maybe it would help if you didn't view society as the interactions of individuals. It's bigger than that." She paused. "Try to imagine all the world's political systems as tributaries feeding into a huge river. People are logs. Either they channel the water in the right direction, or they divert it. If too many of the tributaries are diverted, the river is lost. We're trying to make sure that river is always there. *That's* politics."

"That's horrible," I said. "What about free will? What about individuals rising by sheer talent and willpower? You can't eliminate them!"

"Slash, we're working for the good of America. Of *humanity*. That's the truth, plain and simple. I'm sorry you stumbled into it, but there's nothing to do now but go on. I—*we*—need that PED back. You know how important it is, all the trouble it could cause. So how about coming back to my office and working something out with me?"

I laughed at her. "I'm not crazy enough to do that. You'd kill me the second you had the PED!"

Her face hardened; her lips drew back in a sneer. "I thought we could do this the easy way," she said, "but I see we can't. Fine. I can deal with you on any terms you choose. If you want to play power games, how's this one: we picked up your kit last night."

"You wouldn't hurt him," I said, not believing it.

"He'll be dead this evening. I signed the papers myself. *Unless* . . ."

Stunned, I didn't know what to say, to do. *"Unless what?"* I cried.

She smiled. The whole universe seemed to be narrowing down to her face. Her smug, self-satisfied, self-righteous face. I longed to kill her as I'd never longed to kill anyone before. But I couldn't, not with Jeffy as her prisoner

Then she looked over my shoulder. Her eyes windened, and she took an involuntary step back.

A shadow fell over me. I blinked, looked up, caught a blur of gray. *Hangman*. Jan Harris tried to run, but he was on her fast, steel claws out, ripping, tearing in his fury. Blood sprayed. His weight carried them to the ground.

Then Hangman reared, letting out a primal roar of triumph.

I stared, horrified, as something bubbled in the hole that had been Jan Harris's throat. With a final gurgle, she lay still.

13

I turned on Hangman, enraged, betrayed. "Are you crazy?" I demanded. "She had Jeffy!"

"So?" Calmly, he sat. "It was a trap."

My hands trembled in frustration. When Hangman began to lick the blood from his claws, I longed to strangle him, to choke the life from his body. But I couldn't. He would have ripped out my throat as easily as he'd ripped out Jan's.

I couldn't escape the feeling that I'd lost Jeffy forever. Staring at the body before us, I wondered what might have come of bargaining with Jan, whether she'd really meant to kill me when I surrendered my PED. I'd never know. But I would've taken the chance.

Then I remembered how hard her face had been when she'd betrayed Robert, when she'd shot him in Paris. *She didn't care for life*, I reminded myself. *She wanted the PED back at any cost—and didn't care who she killed to get it.*

"Perhaps you're right," I said somewhat stiffly. "But we'll never know, will we?"

He continued licking himself clean. I took a deep breath. Was it asking too much for cooperation? *There's no looking back now*, I told myself. At least I had Jan's files. They would give me a place to start, and perhaps clue us on how to get Jeffy back.

Hangman finished cleaning himself, then stood, muscles rippling like steel bands. We couldn't stay here much longer, I knew; no telling when the next aircar would pull into this level and see us.

"Get her under cover," I said.

He bent without protest and heaved Jan's body into the back of the coupe. She slid to the floor behind the driver's seat. You couldn't see her body unless you pressed up close; it would probably be several days before someone found her, and only then by the smell.

I slammed the door and heard it lock. Everything now had a sense of finality about it. For the first time, I realized we'd attacked a nondog—something I'd sworn I'd never do. That I myself hadn't killed her didn't matter. It had been done in my name. I didn't think SecurNet would be all that happy about it when they found out, which they invariably would.

"Coming?" Hangman asked.

I nodded, calm for the first time. "It's just all coming down on us at once, that's all. I *am* sorry about earlier . . . I didn't mean to snap at you like that."

"Okay." He padded back toward his Jag.

Following, I suddenly couldn't help but feel he'd prevented me from making a very bad mistake. Jan had claimed Jeffy was her prisoner, and then my brain shut off and raw emotion took over. Very bad, that, in our line of work. She'd been manipulating me like a master at the game. And it would have worked.

But her death had served some good, at least. Several new thoughts:

One, SecurNet had Jeffy. Bad news, but at least I *knew* we had the worst-case scenario.

Two, one key player had been removed. Without Jan Harris

on top of things, SecurNet might well stall in their hunt for us.

Three, we had her files. I hefted her briefcase and smiled. Somehow, I had the feeling more answers lay buried within.

Then inspiration struck. Did she have a PED too? If Robert had one—

"Wait," I told Hangman. "I want to check something."

I raced back to the coupe. The first key on her keyring opened its door. Pulling her body to a sitting position, I let her head fall forward. Blood dribbled down the front of her suit. Then, carefully, I ran my fingers through her hair, looking for anything unusual. A small patch at the back had a slightly different texture . . . but I didn't feel machinery embedded.

Remembering how Grammatica had flipped open a hidden catch on the severed head we'd brought him, I prodded first here, then there with my fingers. Finally something clicked. A patch of hair slid aside, revealing a shiny metal plate.

That was enough to tell me she had a PED. But then the plate opened and I found myself staring at white skull, bits of metal, tiny wires. I'd seen the insides of my PED before Grammatica stuck it in me, and they hadn't looked quite like this. Jan's implant was subtly different . . . perhaps a later model. Which made sense, if she'd been Robert's superior, as I thought.

I squinted at two tiny A/B microswitches. Extending a claw, I hooked the one to the right and pulled it to its second position. A slot opened. A small disk—perhaps ten centimeters wide and three thick—popped out in my hand.

Quickly I tucked the disk away. I'd been lucky here, too; her PED was a different model than mine. You needed surgery to change data disks with my PED, Grammatica had told me. I wouldn't have to decapitate her, or drag her body back with us.

Wondering if she might not have a second disk, I pulled

the other microswitch. Instantly I regretted it. Something hissed inside Jan's head, and electricity crackled over her PED. I dropped her and leaped back. Little tongues of flames burst out through the disk's slot. And dead though her body was, it began to jerk convulsively, arms flailing.

I'd triggered some sort of self-destruct for The PED, I thought. If she'd been alive, it probably would have killed her, and certainly destroyed any data on the disk.

Kicking her body back to the floor of the coupe, I pressed the door shut. It locked. I watched through the window as her convulsions slowed, stopped. The barest trace of smoke rose from her burnt-out head.

I hurried back to Hangman. When I pulled out the data disk and told him what it was, he nodded approval.

"Grammatica can install it," I said as we climbed into his Jaguar and strapped in. "Let's head there first, before anything else happens."

I put the disk inside my skintights where I could feel it next to my heart. He pushed in the ignition cube, upped power, and off we lifted for the exit.

Getting out of the garage was no problem. The attendant waved us through as quickly as he'd waved us in.

As we entered eastbound traffic, my thoughts kept coming back to Jan Harris. What sort of secrets would her PED disk hold—more assassinations? More murders? More terrorism?

Enough to blackmail SecurNet into letting us go, I hoped. *Enough to save Jeffy*, I prayed.

I opened her briefcase and pulled out various folders. Having everything on paper didn't surprise me; I'd long heard that most of our government's secret files had been converted to hard copy for security reasons. More work for the bureaucracy, certainly, but safer in the long run. With all those bright boys running wild through the world's computer systems, you couldn't keep information to yourself these days.

What *did* surprise me was Jan Harris daring to take these

folders from SecurNet's headquarters. SecurNet never would have allowed it, I thought; she must have done it on her own, to work at home. And I imagined they frowned on supervisors taking company aircars, too. I smiled to myself. Petty crime among SecurNet employees. What had the world come to?

From what she'd said, and what I remembered of her from Paris, Jan must have thought pretty highly of herself. For once, something had worked to our benefit.

The first folder I opened had my name on it. I scanned the brief bio, nodding. Yes, everything correct, from schooling to my apprenticeship with Bluth & Gristman Accounting to original hair color (brown) to sexual preference (female and *homo felinus* these days).

Then I turned the page and discovered an annoyingly complete dossier, right down to information nobody should know but me—personal things from before I'd gone cat that never should have been there but somehow were. Like the time I'd attended an antiwar rally with a girlfriend. I hadn't joined in, hadn't sung the protest songs or signed the petitions being passed around. I'd known better; I hadn't wanted to get tagged as subversive. But SecurNet nonetheless knew I'd attended.

They also had all my school transcripts, and statements from former teachers—right down to Mr. Ezekiel in second grade, the first glitterperson I'd ever met. I didn't remember most teachers' names from that far back, but SecurNet had dug them up, made them talk about me.

And, from more recent times, they'd ferreted out all but one of my personal bank codes. *At least they're not perfect*, I thought gloomily. They'd even traced my operation back to dozens of dogmen I'd robbed.

Suddenly I felt a lot less secure about my life.

Someone—perhaps Jan Harris herself—had scribbled notes inside the folder's back cover: "He's smart—or is it luck?" And underneath: "P. says shrewd."

I smiled a bit. Yes, with Pietr I'd been more than shrewd. Walking out with a canister under my arm that day had been one of the smartest things I'd done throughout this whole affair. Misdirection—the thief's best friend.

The next time I looked up from the file, Hangman was pulling down between buildings, circling toward St. Jude Street and Grammatica's shop. This late in the day, glitterfolk and other nightpeople swarmed at street level, in and among the fancy little boutiques catering to their kind. All those blinking lights and dazzling colors, all the shifting antlike movement below—it felt good to be back.

But as we neared ANIMEN-R-Us, the wrongness all but slapped me in the face. The shop's signs were off, and a pair of little red coupes identical to the ones SecurNet used sat in front.

"They got him," I said numbly. "Get us out!"

Hangman didn't blink an eye. We cruised on, lowering because we'd already started down and changing course would show as wrong. My nerves jittered; I chewed my lip and stared at the coupes.

Closing ANIMEN-R-Us took real nerve. Grammatica had always bragged about keeping his bribes paid, about how the feet took care of him. I guessed even feet obstructionism couldn't stop SecurNet when they wanted something badly enough.

Pietr must have incriminated old Esteban Grammatica, I thought grimly. No telling what they'd used to drag it out of him—perhaps even a psychoprobe. If they 'probed him, he had my pity: he'd be little better than mental jelly for the rest of his life. It was one of the most quick-and-dirty ways of emptying a man of information that the Japanese had come up with during the Three Years War, before we nuked them . . . quite illegal now, but I'd have bet anything SecurNet had the equipment. Whatever, I knew Pietr would never willingly have told SecurNet about Grammatica. As Hangman had said, you don't betray your sources, no matter what.

Hangman took our escape slow. He turned into a garage set halfway up the side of a building. Walls and ceiling closed around us, and he flicked on our indoor lights.

It was a grungy place, full of meters for afternoon parking. Rather than set down, though, he cruised up a couple of levels, then out the far side of the building. We pulled behind a fast-moving transit platform and followed it until St. Jude Street lay far behind. I knew the dogs hadn't seen us.

"Where next?" Hangman asked, abruptly dropping to a slower-moving traffic flow.

"Fishtown, I guess." I couldn't think of a better place. At his house we'd be safe for the night, at least. He'd have wife and kits, and I'd have time to read SecurNet's files and think about somehow rescuing Jeffy. I prayed Jan had been lying when she'd said she'd signed his death order.

An hour later, we set down atop Hangman's house. He had his own security system, even better than mine had been, and it checked safe. After we debarked, I helped pull canvas over his Jaguar 44. Then we took a lift down to the kitchen.

His entire family had gathered there, kits at a fold-out table with holobooks playing—probably homework, I thought as I studied the tangle of lines and mathematical symbols hanging over their heads. Children started calculus so young these days.

His wife, Kim, was chopping vegetables at a counter, knife neatly snicking through onions and peppers. Hangman padded over and nuzzled her briefly.

Seeing him immersed in this charade of domesticity almost made me laugh. Thief and killer, that was my Hangman—not meek little Harry the Housecat, insurance salesman extraordinary.

"How was your day?" he asked.

"Long," she said. "It's nice having you home for a change. I hate it when you travel so much."

He sighed; I got the feeling this was an old argument.

"Dinner in fifteen minutes," Kim told us. "It's pot roast. I hope you like it, Peter. Be sure to wash up, Harry; there's something sticky on your paws."

"Yes, dear," Hangman said.

"And did you hear the news?" she asked us both. "About the murder in the park?"

"What?" That pricked my ears up. Murders in Fishtown were rare; I could only recall a handful in the years I'd lived here, and most of those had been committed by shadowcats in the name of justice. "No, we didn't. What happened?"

"A young cat." She nodded. "Horrible, horrible business. I don't know what Fishtown is coming to. Next thing you know, dogs will be running through the streets in broad daylight!"

"Who was it?" I asked urgently, not quite knowing why. "Did you hear?"

"Some black panther. They found him with his head cut off, I think, though I don't know much more than that. The shadowcats will let us know."

Black panther? I thought, horror growing inside. It sounded too terribly, terribly familiar for coincidence. *And his head cut off . . . like they were searching for a PED?*

Hangman looked at me, and I saw pain in his eyes.

14

"Jeffy—" I said.

It had to be. Shock hit me like a knife to the gut. A lump the size of my fist rose in my throat.

"*No*," I breathed. "*No*."

"I'm sorry," Hangman said, and he sounded like the feet who'd called so long ago to tell me my wife had been killed. "I'm so, so sorry."

Kim looked from him to me and back again, bewildered. "What's wrong?"

"The murdered cat—" Hangman said, stopped.

"He was my kit," I said numbly.

"You don't know who he was," she said. "How could you—"

"I *know*!" I snapped. "It's him!"

I could only blame myself. It came to me now, in a sudden revelation like floodwaters bursting through a dam, how wrong my every move had been. Keeping the severed heads when we discovered them in the canisters. Having Grammatica install one of the devices in me. Killing Jan Harris.

Of *course* SecurNet couldn't let us get away with any of

it. We'd murdered their couriers and stolen their property. Jan's death had merely been the latest in a long series of mistakes, and biggest of the lot. We'd pushed SecurNet into a corner. Of *course* they'd pushed back. Of *course* they'd murdered Jeffy in retaliation.

No, I thought, stopping myself. *That's impossible. Decapitating him and dumping his body in Fishtown would've taken time. If Kim knows, word's been out all afternoon. He must've died well before Jan did.*

Which meant he was already dead when she'd tried to bargain with me for his life. I bit my lip so hard that I tasted blood. I *deserved* the pain, I thought. How could I have been so blind stinking *stupid*? She'd never meant to keep any bargain with me. She'd meant to kill us all to protect the secrets locked in my PED. And I'd almost given Hangman and myself into her hands.

"Slash," Hangman said softly.

Shuddering, I pressed my eyes shut. *And letting Jeffy slip away in lockup weather was the biggest mistake of all*. I couldn't escape blame. *If I'd tried harder—if I'd done things just the slightest bit differently—he would still be alive.* My head ached. My hands shook. *They decapitated him*. Decapitated him!

Thinking back to my wife's death, I went all cold inside. Bad memories threatened to come crashing down and overwhelm me. *It always happens*, I couldn't help but think. *Everything I touch, everything I love, ends up dead or ruined.*

Pain welled inside me, sharp and cruel, and I thought it would never end. Turning, I fled through the kitchen, the dining room. I couldn't stay. I had to get out, be alone. I needed time to grieve, time to suffer, and perhaps time to find some way to redeem myself.

My fault—all my fault—

The front door swung open automatically. I tore through on all fours, sprinting like I had Rex himself at my heels.

No matter how fast I moved, though, I couldn't lose my anger, my despair. I called myself all the vile things in the world, a useless senseless parasite—

"Come back!" I distantly heard Hangman calling. "Slash—"

Tears blurring my eyes, I tucked my head down. I turned at the next corner, turned again, heading deeper into Fishtown. Catmen stared as I passed, a few letting out questioning yowls.

No, no, leave me alone. Breath rasping in my throat, heart burning, still I ran.

Finally I hit a small park. Ground blurred underfoot; bushes whipped past. The sweet smells of earth and grass and growing things swept over me, the spoor of birds and squirrels and all the catmen who had wandered here since last rain.

Stumbling, I collapsed beneath a huge old maple. Sharp pains shot through my whole left side. My body shook. Clutching forearm to belly, hardly able to breathe, hardly able to think, I found myself sobbing helplessly as I rocked. The world seemed to be spinning around and around, and I buried my face in my paws and tried to shut it all out.

I wept for an eternity. Jeffy's face rose like a ghost to haunt me. I heard his voice in the wind, heard his soft footfalls at every side.

But eventually my tears passed, as all things do. Finally I could sit up, see the world again. I felt all hollow inside, and a strange light-headedness filled me, almost as though I floated above the world in a drugmist. The horror and self-pity had leeched out, I thought distantly, leaving only emptiness inside. I still ached someplace deep within, yes, but I could tolerate it now, control it now. That blinding, heart-wrenching, all-consuming *pain* no longer swept over me in tidal waves.

I struggled to my feet. The moon was out, full and bright, and from where I stood I could see the entire park. Across from me, at the other side, kits of all ages wrestled on the walkways, mock-snarling and growling. Parents Stood and watched proudly as first one, then another tumbled to the top of the heap. Plastic claws scratched harmlessly; plastic fangs mouthed ears, tails, throats.

I swallowed. God, it hurt to see them. Memories of bringing Jeffy to parks on nights like this one came rushing back. He'd been twelve when he went cat, so burned out from streeter life that I'd thought his emotional scars might never heal. But good healthy play had done it, pulled him around, molded him into a true catman.

So young, so young . . .

I looked down at myself. Grass clung to my coat; I brushed it away, then took a moment to groom myself. It was habit, really, more reflex than anything else, a nervous motion to fill empty seconds.

Then, more slowly now, I moved from cover. I would not drown in sorrow tonight, I vowed. I would do something, anything I could, to avenge my kit.

With darkness here, all the cats in Fishtown had appeared. They clustered on street corners, prowled the alleys, ran and chased and yowled away the darktime hours. I didn't feel like play and wandered through them, oddly apart, almost an outsider, watching as though for the first time.

How shallow our cat-mimicry, I thought, how fragile our little society. Had I really given up my humanity for *this*? It seemed almost a perversion.

As I wandered, I noticed shadowcats lurking in dark places, watching everyone and everything with their nightsight eyes. *Looking for Hangman and me*, I thought, *and making sure they're obvious, so catkind knows it's safe*. With Jeffy's murder so fresh and brutal, many cats would be edged; shadowcats on duty reassured everyone.

Silently I cursed them and their master. They were part of the problem, I realized bitterly. They had surrendered us to

Rex. It would have been so easy to let us go and say we escaped, to keep catkind pure from dealing with dogs.

I lowered my head. *Poor Jeffy.* My promise to kill Hatter came back, but I dismissed it now, knew it as just revenge-fantasy, impractical in the end. I wouldn't get past Hatter's guards if I tried. I'd probably never even see him again, unless the shadowcats caught me and hauled me before him in chains.

I kept walking.

I must have passed a dozen shadowcats in the next hour. Not one recognized me in my cougar skintights. I strolled with impunity down the center of every street, skirting the occasional cat-game, catching snatches of conversation here and there.

Jeffy seemed the main topic tonight. Little surprise, I thought, considering how quiet Fishtown usually stayed. Nobody knew who he was, of course; his head hadn't been found. The shadowcats (they said) would soon catch his killer. . . .

I almost laughed at that.

Picking a milkbar at random, I entered. I'd been here several times before, but not often enough one of the regulars might recognize me.

Muted light came from holostatues of all the great cats of history: Francis Joseph Dougherty V, a minor senator who'd gone cat in his old age and senility; then Xavier, the first catman, who'd molded all catkind and catlife to come; then, biggest of all, none other than Hatter himself. My lips drew back in a sneer. Yes, great Hatter with his kindly shadowcats, protecting Fishtown and all catkind. They hadn't saved Jeffy. They'd helped kill him.

Huge pillows had been piled along the wall to the right of the door. I flopped down on one, calling my order. The milkbar's owner, an old lynx named Smitty, hurried to set a bowl of warm, seventy-proof-alcohol-sweetened milk before me. He paused a moment, squinting when I thanked him, but failed to recognize me. I didn't volunteer a name. When he moved on, I turned to my milk and lapped a bit, listening.

They were talking about Jeffy in here too. How his body had been found, what it had looked like, who might have done it. Dogs, they were muttering. Had to be dogs. Who else could be so cold-blooded?

Shadowcats, I almost said. *SecurNet*. But I didn't.

I finished my milk quickly, left. If I heard anything more about Jeffy tonight, I thought I might cry again.

So much for brutal, uncaring Slash the Outlaw. When my wife and children died, I'd sworn never to love anyone else ever again, and hardened myself against all those soft, weak, oh-so-painful emotions. I'd meant it, too.

But Jeffy had healed all those old wounds, softened all those old scars. And now it hurt all the more because I could have—*should* have—saved him. His death had been so, so unnecessary.

A church bell began to toll . . . midnight, prime time for catkind. The moon passed behind clouds for a second, and I felt adrift from the world.

Around me, in the darkness, games began in earnest. I found myself strolling through teams playing hunt and seek, or tag, or chase. Feet padded lightly, steel nails clicking; nightsight eyes gleamed. Tigers, calicos, cougars, panthers, leopards, lynxes, manxes, ocelots, mountain lions, African lions, tabbies—everyone had come out tonight. Questioning mews carried through the stillness as old friends gathered, new acquaintances met, teams assembled, rules were discussed and agreed upon.

Wandering aimlessly, thoughts jumbled, I stopped paying attention to where I headed. Eyes down, I almost walked into a large brown panther, and that brought us both up short.

"Excuse me," I said automatically, skirting him. His tail

twitched in annoyance, but he nodded and went on without
a word.

Then I caught a whiff of pheromones. He reeked of them,
as Hatter had. My heart began to pound.

Pheromones.

I almost snapped to attention. And then it hit me.

Hatter.

I'd always heard he went out late at night, catching catkind's moods. Part of how he kept hold on reality, they said.
But I'd never seen him out, never run across anyone who'd
met him by night, and figured it had been a lie.

But that panther . . . he'd been large enough, and he'd
smelled right. I'd never met another cat who put out pheromones as Hatter did. *It has to be him*, I thought, looking
back, eyes narrowing to slits. *He disguised himself.*

That made sense. If I could pass undetected just by changing my skintights and dying my face-fur, so could he.

Turning left, I jogged up a narrow alleyway, then turned
left again and paralleled his course. When I cut back fifty
meters later, I found he'd stopped to watch a game of tag. I
paused in a doorway, waiting. When he finally moved on, I
followed, slipping between streetlights, keeping well back.

Half an hour and I knew he wasn't being guarded. The
king, safe in his homeland, secure in his disguise, had gone
out among his people alone and unarmed. I smiled grimly at
his conceit. We had little crime here; under normal circumstances, Hatter would've had nothing to worry about. And if
people wanted him dead, who would recognize him as panther? He lived and worked and played among the shadowcats;
to catkind in general he was just a face on the vid, exotic as
the fabled whale.

Hatter joined a game of hunt-and-seek. As the hunter stood
counting off, players split up. My luck ran wild—Hatter
turned and headed up the alley toward me.

Still I hung back behind garbage cans. *Not yet, not yet*, I thought. Holding my breath, I pressed my eyes closed so they wouldn't catch the light and give me away.

He passed bare meters from where I crouched. I didn't know whether he'd seen me or not, but I doubted it. I squinted after him.

When he turned the corner, I rose and followed. I'd played here before; I knew this area like the back of my paw. He'd turned into a narrow little cobblestone street with buildings on one side and an old cinder-block wall on the other. I leaped atop the wall in a single motion. Gardens lay on its far side, full of fireflies and chirping crickets, and beyond the gardens lay dour old row houses. The thick, rich smell of honeysuckle cloyed around me.

Spurred by adrenaline, I trotted after Hatter. Every sense —eyes, ears, nose—seemed preternaturally sharp, and I thought he must hear me coming. But he didn't. Trees from the gardens overhung the wall in places, dripping grapevines and ivy, and I drifted beneath them like a phantom.

Finally next to Hatter, muscles tight, claws out, I sprang.

He never saw it coming. I hit his shoulder, knocking him off his feet, and had steel claws at his throat before he could scream. He gaped up at me, and I smelled his fear.

"What—" he began.

"Ssst!" I hissed, letting claws prick through his skintights to his throat. "You haven't forgotten me already."

"Who?" he breathed. Then his eyes widened. "Slash!"

"I swore I'd kill you!" I said, and tickled his throat again. Old as I was, much as I hated fighting, I took pride in myself tonight. I'd thought Hatter untouchable. Now, I was alone with him in a dark, deserted street . . . I would take great pleasure in watching him squirm. *A thousand lives for Jeffy's*, I thought. *And you're only the second.*

"What do you want?" he asked slowly.

"To kill you. And before that, to watch you suffer!"

"Your kit . . ."

"Yes-s-s." I drew it out and showed him my fangs.

"I'm sorry," he said, as though he hurt inside at Jeffy's loss. "I didn't know. I protect my own, Slash. I would've tried to stop them. But I didn't know they *had* your kit until they dumped him here."

"Don't your SecurNet friends keep you informed?"

"No."

I paused as a particularly paranoid thought struck me. "I haven't found anyone who saw his corpse. Is Jeffy really dead, or is this some SecurNet trick?"

He shook his head imperceptibly. "No trick. My shadow-cats grabbed the body as soon as they saw it. Too gruesome for the masses. He didn't have a head, Slash!" Hatter shuddered, eyes far away, remembering. "We IDed him from handprints."

He's really dead, then. Somehow, I'd known it deep inside.

"Let me up," he said. "We can talk—"

My claws tightened on his throat. He tensed all over, and shut up. I felt him swallow. He'd begun to sweat, the reek from his modified glands and hormones and pheromones making my head swim. But I wasn't done yet, so I relaxed my hold . . . but only a fraction. I wanted a few more answers before I killed him.

"Why did you turn us over to dogs?" I demanded.

He suddenly seemed to realize his life depended on his replies, and the words poured out: "Just politics—I needed their help—they needed mine. A swap—"

"How could you?" I said in disgust. "Dogs are *enemies*. You kill them. You steal from them. You don't make deals. We don't need their help for *anything*!"

He began shaking, and a weird strangling noise came from his chest. Finally I realized he was laughing. Only when I pricked him with my claws again did he seemed to realize how serious I truly was.

"You're naive," he said. "The war between dogmen and catmen is all hype. I can't believe you fell for it."

"I hate dogs," I said grimly. "*All* dogs. I hated them before I went cat. It's one of the reasons I *went* cat!"

"Your family—" he said, as though remembering something from my file.

"It seems to me," I said slowly, judge pronouncing sentence, "that you've betrayed catkind." I took a deep breath and flexed my fingers, preparing to rip his throat out. Suddenly I didn't care if shadowcats got me. Without Jeffy, I had nothing more to live for. At least with Hatter dead, with Jan Harris dead, my kit would be partly avenged.

Hatter must've felt it coming. He gasped, "Don't you care about *why*?"

I paused. "What do you mean?"

"We can't openly cooperate with dogs, much as I'd like to, because of SecurNet. We have a lot in common with dogmen—more with them than the rest of humanity."

"Go on."

He licked his lips. "Animen are a minority. There are less than half a million of us in the world. If we worked together, we might gain a measure of political power. That's where SecurNet comes in. Their job, their *real* job, is eliminating threats to America's status quo. Organized animen would be just such a threat. Do you understand what I'm saying?"

"I think so," I said, not liking it.

"As long as we're fragmented and fighting among ourselves, we're not a danger. We've got to keep it that way. Most animen would revert to human instantly if SecurNet and the feet started harassing them every time they left their ghettos."

"Sometimes it's easier to give in."

"Or," he said sharply, "SecurNet could go further. They could outlaw animalforms altogether. I don't want that. I'm a cat, and I mean to stay a cat."

"There must be another way," I said.

"We—Rex and all the other animal leaders and I—we've spent twenty years looking, but we haven't come up with one yet." He paused. "So when SecurNet asks, we cooperate. We don't do it willingly. We have to. That's the only way our life-style will survive."

I moved aside, letting him stand. Suddenly I didn't feel like killing him anymore. Suddenly I had a lot more to think about.

"They're looking for something called a PED," he added. "They claim you've got it. They need it back at all costs. If they don't get it, they're going to take reprisals against all animalkind."

"They would, too," I said, thinking of Jan's face as she shot Robert in Paris. *So hard. All killers.*

"Do you still have it?" Hatter asked softly. "Can you get us the PED?"

I still didn't trust him, though I thought I'd begun to understand him a little. Slowly I shook my head. "No," I said. "They took it hours ago. One of their supervisors—her name was Jan Harris—promised to let Jeffy go in exchange for it." I let my voice choke. "Promised—"

"I know her," he said. "A real human bitch."

I said, "Except Jeffy . . ."

"Yes," he said softly. "I'm sorry, Slash. I wish I could've stopped them. I wish I could've done *something*."

I turned and walked away. I'd leave him alive, I thought. His work seemed much harder than I'd ever thought, and much more important. I didn't envy it. He protected catkind all right, but not from dogs, from SecurNet. His was a balancing act between forces trying to pull catkind apart. And suddenly SecurNet struck me as by far a greater threat than dogs.

Suddenly a shrill, piercing whistle rose behind me, hanging in the air. It cut through my head like fingernails on slate.

I whirled, claws out.

Hatter held a little silver tube. He raised it to his lips and blew again, as long and hard as he could.

I cursed. Shopkeepers used whistles like that to call the shadowcats.

15

After a shocked pause, I tucked my head down and ran.
My life depended on speed, I thought. I might have gone
after Hatter, wasted precious time killing or hurting him, but
I knew his shadowcats would certainly catch me if I did.
They came *fast* when that whistle blew.

I'll be back for you later, I mentally snarled at him. My
face hardened. And if I'd shown Hatter mercy before, next
time I certainly wouldn't. His death would be as horrible as
human mind and steel claws could make it.

Seconds later, I hit pavement. When I risked a glance over
my shoulder and didn't see Hatter following, I deliberately
slowed, turning a different direction. I remembered what
Hangman had done in front of Grammatica's shop yesterday:
kept his pace slow, looked like he belonged, and ducked out
the first chance he got. Good strategy.

Behind, the whistle's summons rose again. Two shadowcats, large and silent, hurtled past on their way to answer. *I
don't have much time*, I thought uneasily. How long would
it take Hatter to brief them?

I picked up my pace, trotting now, fast but not suspiciously so. Behind, the whistling stopped. Those shadowcats must have arrived. Two minutes until their search started? Three? Would they remember passing a cougar on their way to Hatter?

Changing directions again, I circled toward the residential section where I'd lived with Jeffy. I wouldn't dare enter my house now; SecurNet doubtless had it wired, and the shadowcats would if SecurNet didn't. But I knew my way through the tall, jutting houses in this part of Fishtown best of all. Here, I could lose anyone tracking me.

I paused, breathing hard. My talk with Hatter had left me curiously refreshed, I realized. Even though he'd tried to grab me, even though Jeffy's loss still gnawed deep inside, I felt young and strong and full of faith again . . . *renewed*, somehow, if that made sense. Hatter had shorn up my crumbling beliefs about the way things ran. Hatter and the shadowcats hadn't sold out to SecurNet. They'd been forced to cooperate.

More pieces were starting to fit together. I thought I knew why we'd been turned over to Rex: after the shadowcats installed SecurNet's tracer in Jeffy's ear, they were supposed to let us go. Instead, Hatter and Rex cut a secret deal of some kind and took a stab at winning the PED for themselves. Perhaps they'd planned to blackmail SecurNet if they got it. Whatever, it hadn't worked, and I now knew Rex's loyalties lay with his own kind first and foremost.

Hatter, though, seemed to be playing both sides against each other. It rankled me that he'd summoned shadowcats after our talk. Bad manners, after I'd so graciously spared his life. What did he intend to do, turn me over to SecurNet anyway? I knew now I couldn't trust him under any circumstances. Even after assuring him I'd surrendered my PED, he'd played dirty.

He couldn't have known I'd lied, of course. And considering the circumstances, he should have given me the benefit of the doubt.

When next we met . . .

I reached my old section of Fishtown without incident. I seemed to have successfully escaped Hatter, but I wasn't taking chances. As I strolled down a winding tree-lined street, I kept an eye out for shadowcats.

My spirits were still running high. Every motion exhilarated me. I had a bounce in my step that hadn't been there in many years. My senses prickled with an unusual sharpness. The *tap-tap-tap* of claws on asphalt, the rustle of leaves in the trees, the distant calls of catmen; everything seemed new and fresh. I felt truly *alive*, and for the first time in quite a while I appreciated it.

I squinted up side streets, my nightsight turning everything to shades of red and pink. I picked out dim inhuman shapes, trashbins and parked landcars, a scattering of kits' toys, and here and there cats tagging through the dimness, playing. Once I even passed young lovers nuzzling among the shadows. I smiled to myself.

Since I didn't feel like returning to Hangman's house yet, I crossed to the far side of the street, where a dozen or so catmen busied themselves knocking a cloth-sewn rubber ball between them. It smelled of catnip, and I paused, catching the sharp scent, savoring it, letting it send my blood racing.

The cats opened their circle without being asked, and I filled the hole. For the next hour I bounced, swatted, kicked, and rolled the ball to other players, losing myself in the rush of the drug and the invigorating pleasures of playtime.

Occasionally I would glance up to note shadowcats passing like bad dreams. They seemed intent on some mission . . . so much so that they hardly noticed me. Not that one tan cougar stood out among so many; in our circle alone, two others fit my description. Ours was a common catform.

Finally one player hit the ball too hard. It skittered through the circle and half a block down the street. In the pause while she went to retrieve it, I thought again that I should've killed Hatter when I had the chance. My fingers flexed as I remembered claws on his throat.

He shouldn't have betrayed me. After I'd given in, let him persuade me of his good intentions, what did he have to gain? *Nothing*, I thought. He just had that mean shadow-cat anger inside, a lust for revenge. Old though I was, fugitive though I was, I'd still found him out, crept up on him unseen, and overpowered him. That would be quite an embarrassment if anyone found out. His pride could never allow it.

Or, I thought, old paranoia creeping back, *perhaps he did have something to gain.*

What if he *knew* SecurNet didn't have the last PED? What if he *knew* Jan Harris had been murdered?

I swallowed. *Then he would've tried to capture me.*

But he wouldn't know that unless he was working for SecurNet. Would he?

It poked holes in all my nice, reassuring theories.

As soon as I could, I left the ballgame and joined a knot of cats heading toward the section of Fishtown where Hangman lived. They too were discussing Jeffy's murder, and I wondered that catkind couldn't find anything better to occupy its time. Hearing the same gory details over and over again depressed me. I almost told them to shut up and talk about something healthy for a change, but that would've attracted attention I didn't need.

At least this group's conclusions were novel: they thought some crazed religious cult had snatched him for an animal sacrifice. And then, considering SecurNet, I wondered if they might not be partly right after all.

About then I caught sight of Hangman walking slowly

toward us, glancing down first one alley then the next. I abandoned the cats and joined him.

"About time," he said, sounding faintly annoyed.

"Sorry," I said, "but I needed to be alone. I think I've gotten everything more or less sorted out now. It all just built up inside me till I thought I'd explode!"

He nodded and turned back for his house. A comfortable silence fell between us, and I thanked him for that. I felt his sympathy, his understanding. Much as he played the brute, I knew he had a lot more inside.

Finally we reached his door. Then I stopped him on the steps and, in a low, urgent voice, filled him in on everything that had happened to me that night. When I repeated Hatter's story about animalkind and its ties to SecurNet, every word rang true. I knew he hadn't lied. Then I told of letting him go only to have him whistle for his shadowcats.

That puzzled Hangman as well. "Should've killed him," he said at last.

I grinned. "You're the muscle."

"So bring me next time!"

His wife and kits were long asleep, but he scrounged a cold supper for me anyway. After I'd eaten, I found I still hadn't come down from my adrenaline high; I was primed for action, ready to track Hatter down again, chase dogs, wrestle shadowcats barehanded.

Then Hangman yawned, showing more teeth than I cared to think about. "Sleeptime," he said. I glanced at the clock and agreed: almost four in the morning.

After washing the dinner bowls, we climbed toward the second floor. I didn't much feel like sleep, with my nerves so keyed, but knew I'd need it.

I said, "Any chance of a sleep capsule?"

"In the drawer," he said, and went down the hall to join Kim in their den.

I closed the door to my room. Opening the night table, I discovered a sealed pack of sleepcaps inside. Flopping down on my pillows, I punched one out, cracked it, and breathed its faintly luminous mist.

The room hazed out of existence.

The next thing I knew, Hangman was shaking me awake. Mine had been a sleep both deep and dreamless; all the better, I thought. After my wife's murder, I hadn't slept well for months . . . I kept seeing her lying in the turbostation, staring up at me with dead eyes and asking, "Where were you, dear?"

Yawning, I rose. From the way sunlight slanted through the windows, it had to be afternoon.

"Brunch?" Hangman asked.

"Five minutes."

He left, and I began rubbing my eyes and stretching. One problem with sleepcaps: they knocked you so far out, you didn't move normally. About half the time I used them, I woke aching from stiff muscles. Not today, luckily.

I dropped to the floor, shifted to catform, and stifled another yawn. The world seemed distant, I thought, very muted; aftereffect of the capsule, no doubt.

Eventually I got myself downstairs. Hangman had served up a dozen bowls of food, everything from eggs to potatoes to fish to three flavors of milk, one heavily laced with caffeine. It was a help-yourself-to-anything sort of meal, and we both dug in with appetites.

Halfway through, I asked about his family. It turned out his kits were in school and his wife was at work. He'd been up for quite some time, it seemed, thinking about yesterday's big find: the data disk from Jan's PED. I agreed with him on its importance. We had to find out what it held before anything else happened. Since Hatter knew we were back in Fishtown, chances were good that SecurNet knew as well.

"What first, then?" Hangman asked.

"We should check ANIMEN-R-Us," I said. "Hopefully Grammatica bribed his way out of trouble, but if not, we'll find another bodyshop. I figure most any of them can install it. The trick's going to be getting out before SecurNet finds us, or before the bodyshop-techs become suspicious and make calls to check our hardware."

He nodded, wiping his whiskers clean. "Let's go."

An hour later found us cruising down St. Jude Street like we had all the time in the world, just another carload of dayworkers on our way to the factory. *No, not dayworkers*, I thought, remembering we were in Hangman's Jaguar. *We're early glitterfolk, spending the day shopping for new mods*.

Uniformed dayworkers filled the street, on their way with mechanical precision to or from factories and company stores. Here and there moved tiny bands of streeters or glitterfolk, oddly subdued and out of place by daylight.

I glanced up. A blue-gray dome of sky, sun peering between buildings like a giant blazing eyeball, not a trace of cloud to be seen. A beautiful day all the way around. No sign of the smogbanks from two nights before; or perhaps this section of the Sprawl hadn't been so badly hit as the one in which we'd been caught.

We neared Grammatica's shop. The neon lights weren't on, of course, but it was daytime and I hadn't expected to see them. One good sign: no red coupes.

Hangman slowed, dropping lower. I thought I glimpsed an Open sign in the main display windows. Then two penguinmen waddled out, looking faintly ridiculous in their black-and-white feathered skintights. Humans, I thought, were never meant to mimic birds. Whatever tech dreamed up penguin mods should be banned from animalform business for life.

"Well?" Hangman asked.

"Set down," I said, smiling for the first time that day. "We're in luck."

Hangman circled the block once to make certain. I took a good look, but caught nothing unusual. Just ANIMEN-R-Us, doing business as usual. I saw neither dogs lurking in nearby alleys nor red coupes stationed on neighboring rooftops. Nothing unusual anywhere.

Still, I thought, considering everything we'd been through, a trap here didn't seem all that unlikely. They clearly knew about Grammatica; wouldn't they have taken precautions in case we returned?

"Find a place a couple of blocks away," I said. "We'll walk."

I wasn't taking chances. Losing Jeffy had taught me that much, at least.

Hangman cruised into a parking building and found a space. As he keyed the Jag's security system to operation, I fed five hundred 'dollars into the meter. It chirped happily and told me I had three hours.

"Thanks," I said sarcastically. Prices were getting crazy in the Sprawl. I could remember when five hundred would've gotten you all of an afternoon.

We climbed down a ramp to ground level. As we neared the smogguard, Hangman tossed me a plastic-wrapped package the size of an egg.

"What's this?" I asked.

"Open it."

I pulled the seals, and to my delight discovered a pair of nose filters inside. He'd remembered how much the centerSprawl airmix bothered me, and he'd even found my brand.

"Thanks," I said, grinning like a kit with new fangs. I pulled out the filters and pushed them in place, breathing deeply. The acrid taste in the back of my mouth vanished when clean air filled my lungs.

We reached the exit. Static crackled around us, and we were out. I paused a moment, squinting into the brightness, getting my bearings. On the corner sat a vidphone booth. I beat a straight line for it.

We had to wait for a dayworker to finish a call, but he eventually cleared out. As Hangman stood guard, I slid into the seat, closed the doors, and fed bills into the slot. Then I punched Grammatica's number from memory.

Two rings later, I found myself looking at Paul's face. "Woof?" he said. "Animen-R-Us."

"Boss in?" I said.

He didn't recognize me as cougar. "Can I help, gentle-cat?" he asked. "He's with some penguinmen right now."

"Why so many penguins these days?"

"Family reunion. Everyone's going as penguin."

I shook my head. "Stupid."

He laughed, tongue hanging out. "Cash customers."

"Doesn't matter, I guess. I'm just glad to see you open. I tried to stop by yesterday for new mods, but . . ."

"A routine crackdown." He shrugged. "Everything's back to normal today." He glanced at something in front of him, studied it, looked back at me. "The master doesn't have any cat-jobs scheduled. Are you sure he's the bodyman you want?"

"Oh, yes," I said with a tight grin. "I'll be there soon." I tabbed off the 'phone, collected my change, and stood.

"It's clear," I told Hangman.

We dropped to catform, padding side by side toward Grammatica's place. Another pair of penguinmen were just leaving. We pushed past them into the cool, dim interior of the store. Somewhere in back, a bell jangled cheerfully.

Nothing had changed. Animal parts still bubbled in the chemtanks along the walls; vid displays still showed the best and the brightest in modern animalforms. Even SecurNet couldn't shut Grammatica down.

Paul came through the shimmerscreen on all fours, tail wagging. "Sit down, sit down," he called, bounding over. "The master will join you in a moment. Just a last few details to take care of, then—"

He abruptly shut up when I pulled my nose filters. He had an odd, suspicious look on his face, and squinted uneasily. Suddenly his eyes widened.

I held up my hand and gestured for quiet.

Slasher? he mouthed silently. Then, looking next to me, *Hangman*?

I nodded, pulling my computer and switching it on. It went through a rapid series of searches and came up green; SecurNet hadn't wired the place, or Grammatica had cleared their bugs.

"Okay," I said, "The place checks. Now, I have some questions about last night."

"SecurNet!" he said. "Looking for you!"

"I know, I know. We were coming here, but saw them and backed off. What happened?"

"Horrible," he said, shivering a bit. "It was a full-scale raid, complete with feet backup. They crashed the doors and stormed us. But Grammatica had gotten tipped, of course, and buried all the hot stuff they might want."

I nodded. *The snakeman's bribes worked*. "Go on."

"SecurNet's boss was pissed," Paul went on. "He came himself and yelled at people. So they copied and photographed and searched everything and everywhere, then hustled Grammatica out for private interrogation." He smiled proudly. "But even SecurNet didn't dare bother *him* much!"

"That's even better than I'd hoped!"

"I'll tell him you're here," Paul said, and bounded through the shimmerscreen happily.

I sat while Hangman paced. *Back in safe territory*, I thought, feeling happier. Grammatica would get that new disk installed. Then we'd have a second tool against SecurNet.

For the hundredth time, I wondered what memories someone like Jan Harris would have saved. She'd been a SecurNet supervisor; nasty secrets, no doubt.

The shimmerscreen crackled, and from the corner of my eye I noted Paul coming in. He moved on two legs, which struck me as odd. I glanced up—

—and found a sleek black projectile pistol leveled at my chest.

"Sorry, Slasher," he said. "I've got to take you in for SecurNet. You and Hangman are burning."

I gaped, too stunned to move. Hangman stopped pacing to crouch, tail lashing. A growl rolled deep in his throat.

"None of that!" Paul said sharply. He licked human lips, took a step forward. "I'm sorry, Slasher, honest I am." He gestured vaguely behind him. "But I owe Grammatica *everything*. They would have shut him down for good if I didn't promise to grab you."

"You don't have to keep your promise," I said softly. "They'll never know we came and went."

"They're going to deep hypno me once a week."

"Grammatica can fix you up, get you psychoscreened—"

He shook his head slowly. "I like you, I really do. But this isn't play anymore. You went beyond robbing dogs. You screwed the *government*. If we don't cooperate, they'll *kill* us. Or worse." He cocked the pistol. "Don't move. Wouldn't want you dead. Not that it matters to *them*."

16

The shimmerscreen crackled again, and this time Grammatica bulked through. He looked as if he'd had a long day already, eyes bloodshot, face sweaty. But he didn't miss a thing. He took one look at Paul holding that pistol on us and bellowed,

"What the *hell* do you think you're doing?"

"Keep out of this," Paul said, glancing over. "It's for your own good."

"It's us," I told Grammatica, "Slash and Hangman. He says he's going to turn us over to SecurNet."

"He most certainly is *not*." Grammatica took three quick steps and grabbed Paul's arm, yanking it back.

Paul yelped, startled, and tried to jerk free. Grammatica merely grunted and set his feet stubbornly. His arm lost its rigid shape and became a python, wrapping around Paul's hand time and again, crushing.

Paul's face grew white; his lips drew back and his face contorted from pain. I heard bones crack.

Then the pistol went off. Its shot reverberated in the small room, loud as a cannon, and I heard a meaty *thunk* like brick hitting flesh.

Grammatica's left eye had vanished, just *gone* suddenly, and the back of his head pulped. I stared in horror as blood and flesh and little chips of bone sprayed the far wall.

''Master—'' Paul cried desperately.

For a long moment Grammatica didn't move, like an insect caught in amber. Then he began to collapse almost in slow motion, bones suddenly gone loose and unjointed. He fell in a heap and didn't move.

I couldn't believe Paul had done it, couldn't believe he'd murdered Grammatica. Paul stood staring dumbly at his master. The pistol dangled from his hand, forgotten.

Now's our chance, I thought, focusing on the pistol. I tensed to leap.

But Hangman had already pushed himself to action. Deathly silent, he glided past me and sprang at Paul.

Paul whirled instinctively, arm coming up with the pistol. They were both moving too, too quickly.

Hangman roared, an angry wail of sound, full of defiance. Then he hit, tumbling Paul backward, and again I heard a sharp *crack*, followed by that *whump* like brick on flesh.

Yowling, Hangman twisted. Something wet splashed my cheek. I wiped at it and came up with bloodstained fingers. *Hangman—*

But he tore into Paul again, madder than ever, biting and clawing as though he hadn't been touched. The pistol clattered across the room and Paul shrieked, no longer fighting but curled into a tight fetal ball, trying to hide, trying to cover himself. Hangman kept ripping like a maniac. Nothing could stand against those steel claws.

At last Paul lay unmoving. His throat, I noted distantly, was mostly gone. Spearlike bones and cartilage jutted from his smashed chest, and intestines trailed from the ground-up meat that had been his stomach.

I had never seen anyone quite so thoroughly dead.

Still snarling, Hangman rose manlike. Blood soaked his skintights, dripping from hands and face. He looked at me and abruptly grinned through that mask of gore.

Taking a step, he started to fall. I raced forward and caught him, eased him down. The bullet had pierced his side, I saw. He had at least two broken ribs. But the hole went through cleanly, at least, and he wasn't coughing blood, which meant his lung hadn't been punctured.

"Got him," Hangman whispered.

"You always do," I said.

And then his eyes glazed and he was out of it. I found his pulse: strong and steady. Just down from pain.

I took a labcoat from the corner rack and tore strips from it, pressing them against Hangman's side to staunch the bleeding. Then I hurried to the front door, locked it, and switched the window's sign to closed. I didn't need penguins wandering through and finding bodies.

Next I went to Grammatica. He kept the keys to his supply lockers around his neck, I remembered. I might not be a medic, but I knew enough about animalforms and plastiflesh to get Hangman's side patched, and enough about drugs to keep him from feeling his wound. Afterward, I'd get him cleaned and to another bodyshop. They'd replace his ribs fast enough; I had ready cash for that.

Grammatica lay on his back, thankfully; I didn't want to see the other side of his skull, the little left of it. His face was bad enough, with the empty socket of his left eye gaping at me. Blood trickling down his cheek.

As I leaned over him, though, I heard a soft, sussurant hiss, vaguely snakelike. His chest rose and fell once, twice, again.

I blinked, startled, somehow terrified. *What*—

I thought to touch his neck. A pulse throbbed beneath my fingertips. It seemed impossible, but he was still alive. With half his skull gone, he was still alive.

His body shivered. His one remaining eye fluttered open.

This can't be happening, I thought numbly. *He's dead. I saw him die. He doesn't have a brain left!*

"I am blind on one side, yes?" he said, gazing at the ceiling.

"Yes," I said automatically. I hesitated. "But how—"

"Bring bandages from the first operating room. Then go to my office. There is a box marked 'Emergency' in the closet. Bring that too." Then his eye closed and he gave a tiny shudder of pain.

Standing, I glanced at Hangman (still unconscious), then turned and darted through the shimmerscreen. Colored light strobed over my eyes. First things first, I thought; my old friend wasn't in any immediate danger.

I trotted down the hallway, the smell of antiseptic strong and sharp, and ducked into the operating room. Bandages lay on a little cart. I grabbed a handful, then hurried to Grammatica's office.

The closet, disguised as a bookcase, stood directly behind the desk. Its secret catch had been smashed (doubtless SecurNet's work), and the door stood ajar.

I all but ripped it off its hinges. Inside, shelves held a clutter of papers and file folders. SecurNet hadn't been very neat in its search, I thought. On the bottom shelf, pushed to the back, sat the box Grammatica wanted.

I dragged it out (it was surprisingly heavy) and hurried to the front room. As I knelt by Grammatica's side, he opened his eye again and focused on me.

"Good job, Slash," he said. "Help me up."

"I'm not sure that's a good idea—"

"Stop wasting time!"

I obeyed. As far as I was concerned, he should have been dead; what did I know about his limits?

When he rose, a stream of half-congealed blood poured from the back of his skull. A thin red line trickled down his cheek from where his left eye had been.

I had to look away, queasy.

He pulled the box closer. Ripping away the top, he rummaged inside, finally pulling out a transparent glass vial marked "Aspirin." Several white tablets lay inside.

"You've got to be joking," I said.

When he pulled the cork, an overpoweringly sickly-sweet smell rushed out, like honey and peach nectar mixed together with huge dollops of sugar.

I gagged, but recognized it: *jumpwire*. Very expensive stuff, designed to kill pain *instantly*. It reroutes most motor actions to the lower spinal cord—faster response time, guaranteed, for anything to do with hands or feet. Too bad it burns out nerves . . . use it more than once or twice a decade and you're as good as crippled. I'd often thought how useful it would be without that nasty side effect.

After dry-swallowing two tablets, a relaxed smile came over Grammatica's face. He wasn't feeling a thing, I could tell. He turned and took in the bloodstained floor and walls, Hangman and Paul's bodies.

"Much better," he said. Gingerly he felt the back of his head. Then he frowned.

Pulling a cake of plastiflesh from the box, he broke its seal and ended up with a mass of soft putty. He reached around and began filling in the hole Paul's bullet had left. He talked all the while, not as though he was in shock, but just pleasant conversation:

"Do not look so sick, Slash. This is no time for neatness, I would say." He chuckled. "I will have a friend do repairs and cosmetics later tonight, when I have a spare hour or two."

I didn't say anything, my thoughts jumbled, confused. The world had taken on some very unreal dimensions, and I thought I must be dreaming. Or nightmaring, really.

When Grammatica finished, he handed me a roll of bandage. "Please," he said.

So I carefully wound gauze around his head, covering up his ruined eye, binding the plastiflesh in place. It would keep the tissue from getting further damaged, I knew, and control bleeding until veins and arteries could be fixed or replaced. At last I finished, and he looked like a refugee from an old war vid.

Slowly, as though every movement took effort, he rose and crossed to Paul's side. He bent to touch the dogman's cheek. I thought I saw tears in his one remaining eye.

"A pity you killed him," he said. "Good servants are so hard to find."

"The bastard deserved what he got!" I said. "He betrayed you, too, don't forget!"

"It was out of loyalty." He said it heavily, as if it pained him. I realized it probably did. He'd always treated Paul like a son. *Like I did Jeffy.* And suddenly Paul's death felt as wrong as Jeffy's.

"He deserved it," I said again, as if repeating the words often enough would make them true. Somehow I didn't sound that convinced or convincing. Away from the heat of the moment, it was easy to forget what Paul had done and recall all the help he'd given me over the years. He'd just been panicked, confused. *If he hadn't shot Grammatica, if we'd taken longer to reason with him . . .*

Grammatica crossed to Hangman. He moved the strips I'd pressed against the bullet wound, then untabbed Hangman's skintights and peeled them back from throat to belly. Bending, he studied the damage.

"He will live," he announced.

"I knew that." I swallowed. "What I want to know is how *you're* alive. Paul put a bullet through your eye, for God's sake!"

"Simple," he said, shrugging. "I modified myself. Not even Paul knew about it. So I must ask you to keep it secret also."

"What—"

"We are in a dangerous business, you and I. People have tried to kill me before, yes, but I have outlived them all." He thumped his chest. "My brain is *here*, behind a solid twelve centimeters of durasteel ribbing. It gets a better supply of oxygen next to my heart, and makes me exceedingly hard to kill."

I stared at his paunch and realized for the first time that none of it was fat. Twelve *centimeters* of durasteel plate . . . you'd need an armor-piercing shell to get through it. On top of his snake mods . . . He'd changed so far from mainline humanity, I wondered if that label still fit.

"What about your head?" I asked.

He smiled. "All this"—he tapped his skull—"is empty now. Everything except the optical nerves has been stripped out. I have mostly muscle tissue here. Simple, yes?"

"Muscle?" I asked doubtfully. Under different circumstances, I would have laughed. Under different circumstances, it would have been funny.

He nodded. "Humans are simply too fragile as built. These modifications have slowed my reactions, yes, but they are better in the long run. And that, my good cat, is what I am in this business for: the long run. Indeed." He wiped at the line of blood running down his cheek from his ruined eye. "Now fetch a cart, Slash. I believe Hangman needs patching?"

Hardly able to believe, I obeyed.

* * *

I got stuck doing Paul's work: prepping Hangman while Grammatica readied himself for surgery. As the snakeman bustled from room to room, rounding up equipment and the replacement parts he'd need, I stretched Hangman out on one of the operating tables.

He came awake with a groan when I peeled his skintights away from the two bullet holes again. Blood made the fabric stick to the wounds, and my clumsiness must have hurt a good deal. Hangman took it all stoically, barely wincing at the worst of it.

When Grammatica walked in, though, Hangman did a double take and stammered, "W-what—?" It was the first time I'd seen him caught completely off guard.

"Don't worry," I said, taking a sleep capsule and breaking it under his nose. "He's only a little dead."

I read bewilderment in his eyes. Then the mist had him and he was snoring softly; Grammatica could begin.

"Slash," Grammatica said, picking up an electric scalpel. It whirred as he made a neat incision across Hangman's abdomen in an alarmingly offhanded manner. "I know how you dislike blood. Will you put Paul in the freezer while I work? I want him unspoiled."

"Sure," I said thankfully, and hurried out.

Somehow, I had a feeling this was going to be one of those days in which everything happens all at once and you scarcely have time to breathe.

I dragged Paul to the cold storage room, where Grammatica kept the most delicate animalform parts and mods, and stretched him out on crates as though on a mortician's slab. Then I went back to the display room, searched until I found mop and bucket behind a tank of vole parts, and began cleaning the floor and walls. Blood was nothing unusual for a bodyshop; any I missed would scarcely attract attention. But I didn't want to leave huge slicks of it congealing here, either. Besides, it felt good to do *something* instead of idly waiting.

As I was just finishing, Grammatica stepped through the shimmerscreen. "Done," he announced. "Hangman will be out in a moment. Is Paul . . . ?"

"Safely chilling," I said. "Why not simply dispose of him in your culture tanks, though? Easier by far."

"I want a DNA sample."

"You're going to clone him? After *this*?"

He shrugged. "I would miss him. I need the help, and with the speedups these days, I can have him full-grown in five years. I will see to his education myself, and make him more useful than before. More discreet this time, yes."

"I suppose."

"Now," he said, pressing palms together, "I believe we have business?"

"Business?"

"You came for something originally," he said. "Yes?"

"Right." And I told about the memories on the first PED, how we found and tracked Jan Harris, how Hangman had killed her and I'd discovered her data disk. He nodded when I described the PED's self-destruction.

"A second-generation machine, doubtless," he said. "Quite interesting. You should have brought it back."

"Not a chance," I said. "After all the trouble we've been through, you don't want to be pulled in deeper. Besides, it burned itself out. I can't imagine it's usable."

Then I told about SecurNet's files, how Pietr's had been marked "Canceled."

"I'm certain he's dead," I added. "And I'm just as certain they'd kill you, too, if they thought you had one of their PEDs."

"Perhaps." Grammatica exhaled slowly. "Pietr disappeared two days ago. His friends are searching for him. Unfortunate, his loss. He was a brilliant man."

"Can you install the new disk in me?" I asked.

"It is compatible . . . ?"

"*I* don't know!"

He smiled, forked tongue flickering across his lips. "We shall see. We shall see." He gestured toward his operating room. "Come."

17

Two hours later, I thought of killing Senator Underhill.

Instantly walls rose before me: a coffee shop of the kind found in large hotels, decorated all in muted shades of gray and green. Plates clinked; silverware rattled. A muted undercurrent of voices registered at the back of my mind, all speaking French.

As I stared through a huge picture window onto a bustling street, I realized I'd watched this scene before . . . only the last time it had been from a different angle, one much higher up.

Across from me towered a huge office complex. I watched a huge black limousine hover slowly into view and land before it. Four men in dark suits climbed out.

Then a knot of people exited the office complex and hurried forward, toward the waiting limo. As they neared, a heavyset man squeezed out. Smiling, he turned and began to extend his hand.

I knew him, of course: Senator Underhill. And I knew what came next: a dull, muted pop, as though from distant fireworks.

Underhill's head pulped, and his body spun once, graceful as a ballet dancer, spraying blood in some comical dance. Then came a brilliant flash of light, so bright I had to glance away, and the plate-glass windows shattered from the shockwave. The people around me dived in all directions, some screaming, some covering their heads, all doing nothing but adding to the confusion.

When I looked back outside, flames leaped twenty meters into the air. The aircar burned, and dozens of people around it lay on the ground and burned too. Some screamed, rolling madly to get rid of the flames, but most were dead already, or soon to be dead. Bits of molten plastic and metal rained down.

I reached down, picked up my cup, and took a long sip; I smelled the coffee but didn't taste it. I seemed to be taking everything with a remarkable calmness, so callous I might have been watching a vid for all the concern I showed.

Others around us began to rise and slowly move toward the broken windows for a better view. I heard excited murmurs in French, understanding none of it, and worked on finishing my coffee before joining the crowds.

As I neared the windows, I caught my reflection in a bit of broken glass on the floor. Jan was smiling like a child with a new toy.

Abruptly I didn't want to watch any more. I willed the memory away, and it switched off like a light.

Blinking, I found Grammatica's bandaged face centimeters from my own. "Yes?" he prompted.

"It works," I said, "perfectly."

Hangman appeared behind him. "Ready to go?" he asked.

I nodded. To Grammatica, I said, "How much this time?"

He gestured vaguely. "Do not concern yourself about it. I will make up a bill the next time you come in."

Of course, I thought. Business was business, even if Paul

had tried to turn us over to SecurNet; what discount did *that* warrant?

I spent the rest of the day holed up in my room at Hangman's house, going through every memory I could find on the PED. Most seemed meaningless to me—just late-night meetings in deserted parking lots. Jan would hand over a satchel, or accept a package; few words were spoken, and those mostly in French or German. To the best of my knowledge, no names were given. Doubtless these memories were important. Why save them otherwise? But I could make no sense of them beyond the obvious: secret payoffs for espionage of some kind. Perhaps they tied in with Underhill's assassination in some way; perhaps not.

Then things started getting interesting. I found myself in the middle of a screaming argument in French. I stood in a morgue of some kind; the wall before me consisted of nothing but little doors. Two stood open, and metal tables extended from them. On the tables lay two sheet-covered bodies. Both had faces showing, and both were quite dead. The one on the right I recognized as Robert; the other was the pinch-faced man.

The morgue attendant was cursing at me. I understood that much, at least. I said something back in a very sweet voice, also in French, then the attendant crossed to a vidphone.

He made a hasty call, spoke politely with a man in black uniform, and finally nodded. When he turned to face me again, his manner had changed. He'd become subdued, so polite as to be almost obsequious.

"Get them," I said in English.

A handful of men moved forward, spread bodybags open on the floor, and lifted Robert and the pinch-faced man into them. After sealing the bags, they carried them through the door. I followed.

Then something went wrong with the memories. Perhaps, I thought, the disk had a flaw. Or perhaps Jan's death had somehow scrambled the data. Whatever, instead of a continuation of the morgue scene, a random jumble of conversations and actions swept over me.

Flash and I stood in a barn or shed of some kind. The two corpses, stiff as boards from rigor mortis, lay on sawhorses. I heard the roar of a chainsaw—

Flash and I stood in an office looking at a gray-haired old man behind a desk. He wore a white suit, and though his expression seemed bland, I got the sensation of deep anger.

". . . mean, you've lost them?" he was saying. "Do you realize what will happen if someone finds the PEDs? If someone discovers what they *do*?"

"Sir," I said, and this time my voice was hoarse, "we think we know who stole them."

"You *think*?"

I nodded. "A group of catmen, Mr. Glass. They make their living by ambushing smugglers."

"I don't care how you do it," Glass said, so softly I had to strain to hear, "but get them back. Or I'll have *your* head in their—"

Flash and we were standing in a dark parking lot—

Flash and I held a smoking gun. Robert lay on the floor, half a dozen slugs in his chest.

I crossed, bent, and made sure he was quite dead.

"Call the feet," I said as I looked back toward the two men who'd helped me murder Robert. "Tell them we got the terrorists who killed Senator Underwood."

"Terrorists?" asked the pinch-faced man on the left.

"That's right," I said. I whipped my hand up, squeezing

off three quick shots. Every bullet hit the pinch-faced man's chest dead on target. He fell without a sound. "You don't think Robert here could do it all by himself, do you?"

"I'll make the call," the other man said grimly, reaching for the vidphone—

Flash and we were strolling down a winding pebble path in some park. Twilight; a warm breeze whispered through the leaves on the trees. I couldn't see anybody else, though I had a peripheral awareness of someone walking beside us, because I kept my attention on the path ahead.

"It's a big step," I said.

"But necessary." I recognized Glass's voice. "He's putting too much pressure on us. He *must* be removed this month."

"Where?"

"France." He chuckled, a nasty sound like grinding rocks. "Rather ironic that he has choosen to attack the organization charged with his safety."

"Any particular time?"

"You'll have ample opportunity. He's making a series of speeches."

"Terrorists again?"

"As always. I want—"

Flash and we were sawing the heads off bodies like branches off logs. Metal canisters stood at hand—

Flash and we were in a vidphone booth, keying a number. Abruptly the screen flickered to life. Glass appeared, frowning. He opened his mouth—

Flash and we were on a beach at night. Sand crunched underfoot; waves hissed. A boat shifted before us, its hull black with radar-absorbing plastic. I recognized it as the one that had dropped off the PEDs.

But, I thought, it wasn't in the Sprawl now. This had to be France.

Two men jumped into waist-high water and waded toward shore. As they neared, I glanced down. Moonlight gleamed off the canisters crooked in my arms—

Flash and I glimped Jeffy's face—
Flash and Glass stood before me—
Flash and—
Flash—

My head ached. I thrust all the memories aside and sat up, rubbing my temples.

Jan's memories seemed to be disintegrating the closer I came to her death. I'd been lucky to learn so much.

SecurNet had ordered Underhill's murder . . . specifically Jan's boss, a man named Glass.

Jan had shot both Robert and the pinch-faced man. Something must have gone wrong, I thought; perhaps the French feet were too close to catching them and she preferred giving them the bodies of two terrorists. So, under her guise as a SecurNet supervisor, Jan claimed to have tracked them down to a hotel room, burst in to arrest them, then ended up killing them in a shoot-out; very simple. Then she'd used SecurNet's influence to get their bodies before the French authorities could perform an autopsy and discover the PEDs.

Somewhere outside Paris, her men had severed the two heads, packed them up, and made arrangements to ship them back to this country secretly . . . to retrieve either the PEDs or the data disks within them.

And that's where I'd come in. Jan had chosen smugglers to transport the PEDs, most specifically a group partnered with dogmen in the United States. They must have been working for SecurNet on the side; easy money on top of what illegal drugs brought. It had been bad luck, their carrying SecurNet's cargo when I'd ambushed them. Singularly bad luck.

Somehow I had the impression Glass wouldn't stop until he had the PEDs back and us dead. He hadn't hesitated to kill a Senator; why should murdering two catmen bother him?

I remembered the glimpse I'd caught of Jeffy's face. Jan had probably killed him herself, I thought, tortured him for information he hadn't possessed, and which his psycho-screening wouldn't have let him reveal even if he *had* possessed it.

The chase must end, I thought as new tears began to well in my eyes. *Jeffy, Jeffy* . . . I didn't know how much more I could take.

But perhaps I could still work something out. Jan had been hard inside, a fanatic. Glass hadn't struck me that way. Corrupt and without principles, yes. Power-mad, certainly. But not closed off to ideas the way Jan had been. People didn't rise far in SecurNet without more than a measure of cunning.

I'd taken the second PED to get blackmail material. I thought I had it now. Or at least enough to make Glass *think* I did.

It didn't take long to tell Hangman of my plan. He agreed at once and took me down to the basement of his row house.

It had been altered into a large office. He showed me the whole setup, including his direct link to the stock exchange.

"I thought those were for the megarich," I said.

"I am," he said.

And that, I thought, explained the Jaguar 44 on the roof, all the fancy alarms there and in his house, and how he'd managed to set up a second identity and keep it such a secret: all that took a lot of money.

"So why go after dogs?" I asked.

"I enjoy it."

I shook my head, bewildered, wondering what dogs could ever have done to him. They'd killed my family, after all, not his. But when he didn't offer an explanation, I didn't push. He had more than earned his privacy.

Among the office's various high-tech toys I found a wall-size vidphone with scrambler circuit. That one little attachment cost more than I made most years. It sent enough white noise alongside the vid signal to make tracing difficult.

I'd seen Jan dial Glass's number in one fragmented memory. It came back to me when I willed it, and I jotted the number down. Then, motioning Hangman out of view, I made the call.

The 'phone rang. Then the screen flickered to life and I found myself face-to-face with Glass.

He wasn't smiling. And when he saw me, he didn't say a word, just stared.

"I believe we have something to discuss," I said.

"Are you Slash?"

"Yes."

"This is an unlisted number."

"A mutual acquaintance gave it to me." I paused. "I didn't call for games, Glass. There's a scrambler on this line; don't bother tracing. Anyway, I'll be off before you get anything."

"What do you want?" he growled.

"To give you information. First, I know all about Senator Underhill's assassination. Second, I know a good deal about SecurNet's whole Paris operation . . . particularly Jan's part in it. And third, I know enough about your involvement to tip the NewsNets onto a lot of things you don't want aired. If you think Underhill was a threat, you haven't seen anything yet."

I might have been reciting a cake recipe for all the reaction he showed.

"And?" he finally said.

"Everything's getting out of hand. Your people have been chasing me, harassing friends, murdering relatives—"

"Your hands aren't clean."

"We're nowhere near even."

He paused. "About the NewsNets . . ."

"I haven't given them anything yet. Perhaps later. Perhaps not at all. I thought I'd give you a chance to deal."

"I'm listening."

"Meet me in Bristol Park at noon tomorrow. Come alone and unarmed."

"No."

"If you don't," I said, "I *will* go to the NewsNets. And let me tell you, your name *will* feature prominently. Our friend Jan saved memories almost compulsively. I have one in particular that you'll be interested in . . . it shows a certain SecurNet officer ordering her to kill Underhill. Perhaps you remember it? Walking through a park as you both talked?"

"Noon, then," he said suddenly. "And—"

But I'd already switched off the vidphone.

18

In the end, I decided not to return to Animen-R-Us that day. Grammatica needed time to get himself fixed. Eyes are tricky things, and coupled with a skull replacement, I thought he might not be up to further operations, despite what he'd said about the ease of his fix. Besides, he needed time to mourn Paul and start that DNA sample.

Tomorrow would be soon enough. Knowing him as I did, I felt certain he'd be open for business as usual.

When we arrived at eight the next morning, however, the sign in the window proclaimed Animen-R-Us closed. I paused, then realized his normal business hours hadn't started yet. Then, shrugging, I rang the bell. It jangled deep within.

After a minute I heard a stirring. The door cracked, and Grammatica peered out. He looked completely normal, the gray-green scales on his snakeskin head shimmering with little iridescent rainbows, new eye small and black as the old one. I couldn't tell he'd been injured at all.

When he saw us, he opened the door farther. "Come in, come in, yes!" he said jovially.

When we entered, he flipped a switch by the door and the room flickered to life, vid displays on the walls, holos of work he'd done. Something new: half a dozen quarter-sized holos of penguinmen materialized on the floor, waddling this way and that, tumbling like little acrobats.

"Aren't you sick of penguins?" I said.

"I have created over fifty this month alone!"

I shook my head, bewildered. "You should push cat."

"What," he asked, forked tongue darting over thin lips, "can I do for you, Slash?"

"I want you to remove my PED," I said.

"Oh?" His eyebrows raised. "It is malfunctioning?"

"A bit. But that's not why." I spent the next few minutes outlining what had happened. "So," I said, "I need both the PED and two disks stored until after my meeting with Glass. I don't trust him not to grab me. I'm sure he would if he thought he'd get away with it. The disks may be our only bargaining point if he does—and even if he doesn't."

Grammatica nodded. "Should he betray you, I can do more, yes. Pietr had many friends, all bright boys into esoteric hardware like your PED. I have asked. For poor dead Pietr they will gladly convert both disks to something standard."

"Like a vid?" I asked.

"Doubtless an old-style two-dimensional, without full senses. Visual and audio only, I would imagine. Yes."

"Fine," I said. "I don't want it to come to that, but I'm glad to know the possibility exists."

"This way." He took my arm, hand wrapping around it time and again, and led me toward his operating room.

It didn't take Grammatica long to strip the hardware from my brain, and when I woke I didn't feel a bit different. I had no sense of dislocation this time, no pain, no discomfort at all.

"Are you sure it's out?" I demanded.

"Of course." He indicated a little wheeled cart, and there sat my PED. It looked like a tiny metal squid attached to a steel box. Jan's disk lay beside it.

I rubbed my head hesitantly. "How come I don't feel it this time?"

"Your body has not been augmented. There is nothing new to which you must grow accustomed."

"Oh," I said. Then I caught sight of the clock on the wall and yelped. Almost eleven—we didn't have much time before my meeting with Glass.

"Do you wish me to keep the PED for you?" Grammatica asked.

"Yes," I said. "Can you put them someplace safe, in case SecurNet sweeps here again without warning?"

"Certainly."

I swung to the floor and began pulling on my skintights.

We circled Bristol Park twice. Hangman had insisted on borrowing Grammatica's aircar, which turned out to be a black Ford sedan so ancient it belonged in a museum. It didn't even have an autopilot. The snakeman didn't get out much anymore, I supposed; the world came to him.

But his sedan worked perfectly, and got us there on time. And it certainly kept Hangman's Jaguar 44 safe from SecurNet's prying eyes.

Glass was sitting on a bench in the exact middle of the park. A bronze Civil War statue of two clashing soldiers stood before him, and he leaned chin on hand, watching pigeons roost. He wore a plain gray daysuit, gray hat, gray shoes. A cane leaned up beside him.

I didn't see any dogs, or anyone I could identify as belonging to SecurNet, so I let Hangman land on one of the walkways. Illegal, yes, but I felt certain no feet would object today.

After popping the door, I eased out and took another look.

Still safe. Only then did I drop to catform and lope to the bench.

Glass nodded. "Slash, I presume?"

"Of course."

When he nodded again, I sat before him, letting steel claws show. If anything happened, I'd cut his throat before they took me down.

"Let's get to the heart of the problem," he said. "You have something I want. Name your price."

"Here's the deal. I'm willing to turn the PED over to you, but I expect certain things in return."

"Name them."

"I want to be left alone, and I want my friends to be left alone. That means no dogs, no shadowcats, no supervisors like Jan Harris trying to kill us."

"Done," he said.

"And," I said, "I want incontrovertible proof that Hatter is really working for SecurNet."

Glass thought about that for a long time. I let my eyes narrow to slits. This would be the crucial part, I thought.

Finally, almost reluctantly, Glass said, "Hatter has worked faithfully with me for more than twenty years. We do not betray our employees."

"Like the senator who wanted to break up SecurNet?" I said. "Like the two SecurNet assassins Jan killed and gave to the French feet?"

"There are exceptions."

"Make another one."

Another pause. "What are you planning to do?"

"Bring him down."

Glass laughed. "I think you might," he said. "I think you just might. Very well, done."

"And," I said, "I don't want Hatter being tipped."

"That goes without saying."

"I'm saying it anyway."

"Anything else?" he asked.

"That should do it."

He nodded. "I'm satisfied. When do I get the hardware?"

"You can have the PED whenever you want. We'll do a straight trade for the info on Hatter. I'm keeping the two data disks, though."

His eyes widened in surprise. "Oh?"

"I'm not stupid, Glass. They'll be kept in a safe place until I or my friends ever have need of them. But we won't go to the NewsNets unless you make us."

He nodded again, more slowly. "That will have to do." He stood, adding, "Call me at five tonight. I'll have the material on Hatter for you then."

"Done," I said, and we shook hands.

Glass actually kept his word; when I called him, he had everything ready. We just needed to make the exchange. We arranged time and place, and I hung up, satisfied.

After getting the PED from Grammatica, I took a transit platform to the corner of 1000th Street and Broad. Night had fallen by then, and Glass was waiting.

We traded packages, then he tipped his hat and climbed into the little red coupe by the curb. It lifted, and he was gone. I hoped never to see him again. He could put on the charm when he wanted to, but I still didn't trust him.

I hopped the next transit platform, changed at the main station, and soon found myself headed toward Fishtown. I would sleep in my own house tonight, I thought, and on my own pillows.

Now that everything had come to a conclusion, I felt exhausted both mentally and physically. Not a victory exactly, but not a loss either . . . more of a tie, I decided, which was better than I had any right to expect from a tangle with SecurNet.

Poor, poor Jeffy. I would miss him. But at least I would take Hatter down. That much I could do to avenge his murder.

Hangman joined me early the next morning. I pulled the datachip from its case and plugged it into my computer.

The files were clear enough: logs of SecurNet payments to Hatter, reports Hatter had filed with his superiors at SecurNet, missions that shadowcats had run with Rex's dogs, all manner of damning evidence—right down to Hatter's plans to round up catkind should animalforms ever be outlawed.

Nothing criminal or even illegal in the whole batch, of course; Hatter had done everything according to government form. His sins were more subtle: making us think he worked for catkind rather than SecurNet. Making us believe in a war with dogs. The truth would come as quite a shock.

Hangman and I excerpted the most inflammatory files and put them together into short articles. It became almost a game between us. We made ourselves yellow journalists, seeing who could sling the greatest accusations and slur Hatter's name the worst.

HATTER BETRAYS CATKIND!
He's a SecurNet Spy!
READ THIS SHOCKING *TRUE STORY!*

Believe Your Own Eyes
SECURNET OWNS FISHTOWN!
HATTER GOES BERSERK!
Power Has Driven Him Mad.
PROTECT *YOUR* KITS—END THE TYRRANY!

These articles would, I thought, make quite a breakfast read for the morning cats, those with day jobs. I loaded the files into my house computer, tabbed the computer into the 'phone lines, and set my program running.

Electronic mail addresses in Fishtown all share a common first four digits. My computer began dialing Fishtown numbers starting from 2932-00000 and working toward 2932-99999. When my computer reached another computer, it uploaded the files with orders for an immediate printout. A call took only two or three seconds. And the last line of every article said, "Send these files to your friends *at once*. We must stop Hatter *now*!"

Enough catmen would read it, I knew, to get things rolling. Once word spread, once printouts started being passed hand to hand, Hatter would never be unable to stop it.

I smiled to myself, and sat back to watch the explosion.

19

It started slowly at first, with faint rumblings against an ominous stillness, like an avalanche slowly building from the top of a mountain.

Throughout most mornings I'd hear dozens of aircars as neighbors headed to work in the Sprawl. Today, though, a deep silence burred in my ears. Far away, a single aircar thrummed to life. The cat who owned it must have skipped the morning printouts, I thought.

Then my vidphone rang. I jumped, startled, but answered fast enough.

It was Hatter, back in lionform. "What the hell do you think you're doing?" he demanded in a low, dangerous voice. He waved a fistful of crumpled sheets of paper at me, eyes narrowed in fury.

"Beg your pardon?" I smoothed my whiskers and looked smug.

"You know what I mean." He shook the printout. "*This!* It just came over my computer!"

"What makes you think I'm responsible?"

"I'm not stupid, Slash."

I smiled and said, "In that case, I'm just disseminating public information. Don't you *want* to know what's going on in Fishtown?"

He sputtered for a moment. I didn't wait; I switched off the 'phone. When it rang again, I didn't answer. Why bother? It would piss him, and angry he'd make mistakes.

"Let's go out," Hangman suggested.

"Do you think he'll send shadowcats after us?"

He shrugged. "Just out."

So we went to the front door. Word must've spread throughout most of catkind by now. Quite a few cats were up and about, sitting on porches, talking in little groups, passing copies of the articles. I'd never seen so many catmen by day before.

I could hear calls spreading up and down the block, as those who hadn't heard were summoned forth. The air took on an almost tangible undercurrent of tension and anger. I'd felt the same thing during lockup weather. *Violence coming*.

Finally, as though some unanimous but unspoken decision had been made, cats began to drift toward the center of Fishtown, toward Hatter's palace. Perhaps they wanted to see him, I thought. Perhaps they wanted to hear him deny what they'd read.

We joined the growing throng. As we walked alongside the others, I took in the collective mood and liked what I found. These cats, I thought, would turn nasty fast if Hatter didn't appease them. The white lynx next to me summed it up in short, angry words: "He ought to be run out of catkind! We don't need SecurNet traitors! We don't want him here!"

Murmurs of assent came from those around us. More than outrage, I thought. More than anger. They'd been betrayed, and that cut deep. I remembered how painful it had been for me personally when I'd discovered his ties to dogkind. Those around me had trusted him the same way, truly *believed* in him. They were shopkeepers like Smitty who'd hung Hatter's holo proudly on their walls. They were kits who'd grown up idolizing him, who'd always wanted to be just like him, defending catkind from dogs. They were parents and teachers and salesmen and mechanics. They were all the cats Hatter supposedly protected. It *hurt* for them to have their god stripped bare, his every flaw revealed. They wanted his blood.

Hundreds of catmen already massed outside Hatter's palace, and more were pouring in from every direction. Tall, spiked durasteel gates closed off the palace steps; a line of shadowcats stood guard, unmoving as statues and just as hard. They'd been fitted out for a riot, I noticed uneasily, with stunguns and sleepgas grenades. Hatter must have picked up on coming trouble *fast* to have those out already.

The cats around us shifted foot-to-foot, hissing among themselves, working toward a frenzy. I'd never seen catkind so roused.

"Let's see Hatter!" someone shouted.

"Haul the bastard out by his tail!" shouted another.

I drifted to the side, getting a better view of the palace doors. Hangman followed. Hatter couldn't stay in there forever, I thought. That would be the same thing as admitting guilt. He'd lose everything if he didn't at least *try* to talk down this mob.

At last the palace doors swung wide. A dozen shadowcats trotted out, all fitted with riot gear. They went straight to the guards and passed on instructions.

Immediately the durasteel gates were unlocked and pulled open. Shadowcats stood aside as hundreds, perhaps thousands of catmen swarmed into the courtyard and started up the palace steps.

And from within the palace came Hatter himself, looking old and tired. His mane billowed in the wind, and he paused to gaze down on all the cats below.

To a one, they stopped. Hatter still had a measure of stage presence, I'd give him that. I couldn't take my eyes off him. I held my breath in anticipation.

Slowly, regally, Hatter moved forward. He didn't hurry; he might have had all the time in the world. At the top of the steps, he paused and looked across the crowd. Rearing back, he stood manlike. Then he held up his paws for silence, but he needn't have bothered; an expectant hush had fallen.

He was going to deny everything, I thought suddenly. He was going to deny everything, and they would believe him. He hadn't even spoken yet and I knew every word he was going to say.

But at least here, in the open, he couldn't use those leadership pheromones. He didn't command instant respect.

Someone hissed at him. He stared back, almost in disbelief.

Then another cat hissed, more loudly, and the crowd picked it up, the sound swelling, rising like a wave to swamp him. The cats around me began to click their steel claws. The sound grew deafening.

Hatter motioned again for silence. The cats didn't obey, refused to listen. Hatter began talking anyhow, but his voice didn't carry. When he reached to his throat and adjusted something, I realized he had a microphone clipped to his mane. It wasn't working. Glass's work? SecurNet's? It had to be.

I smiled and began clicking my claws too, louder and louder, faster and faster. The noise became an endless crash of sound, metal on stone, metal on pavement, and I knew Hatter couldn't stand there much longer. Catkind's emotions were high, getting wild. Soon they'd call for his blood.

But Hatter wasn't beaten yet. He raised his paws again and shouted his loudest:

"Friends!" I distantly heard. *"Listen to me!"*

Again the cats began to hiss, drowning him out. He shouted something further, but the words were lost.

The shadowcats were moving slowly, I noticed then. Tails between their legs, taking furtive glances in every direction, they slunk to the sides, down the steps, into the crowd. Catkind gave way for them. In a second the shadowcats had fled.

Hatter realized it suddenly. He looked around, but all his guards had fled and he stood alone atop the palace steps. The shadowcats, greatest symbol of his power, had abandoned him, left him unprotected.

"Now!" someone at the fore shouted, and as a single unit the cats charged. Hatter just stood, eyes wide, unable to believe what was happening.

The first cats to reach him pulled him down. I caught a flash of steel claws and a glimmer of bright, liquid red. Then bodies surged and Hatter vanished beneath a writhing mass of catmen. More and more cats crowded closer, trying to see, trying to get at him.

I felt a rising contentment inside. *Now catkind is free,* I thought. *This is for you, Jeffy. May you rest in peace.*

I turned to go, and found myself facing three shadowcats, the largest and meanest set I'd ever seen. I recognized one; he had a jagged scar across his face, puckering his mouth into an endless snarl. He'd used the stungun when Hatter questioned me. He'd turned me over to dogs.

"Hello, Slash," he said, grin widening. "We've been looking for you."

He motioned the other two forward, and they grabbed my arms before I could protest. I twisted to look at Hangman and found four more shadowcats holding him too.

Then suddenly the shadowcats hoisted me onto their shoulders and marched me back toward the palace. I let out a startled, panicked yowl.

"Make way!" scar-face bellowed. He drew his stungun and began shocking catmen too slow to move. "Make way for the new head of Fishtown!"

20

"Put me down!" I shouted. **"I'm not the head of anything, and I don't want to be!"**

But they wouldn't listen. They carried me up the steps on their shoulders, proclaiming me the new leader of catkind every inch of the way. Still I tried to deny it.

As we neared the top, something sharp bit my leg. I howled in sudden pain and twisted around. A drugtab fell away. Then my mouth went dry and I smelled an overpowering strawberry smell, and I knew what it was: *bliss*.

After that, my mind turned to jelly. I began smiling, deeply contented, willing to go along with anything. *Let* them make me emperor of Fishtown. Terrific! More fun! I laughed happily.

They were holding me up before the crowd of cats. Scarface was talking, but it barely registered. Something about my "having revealed the corruption in Hatter" and my "leading the reform movement."

The cats all cheered. I smiled distantly and waved. And then the shadowcats carried me into the palace and the doors shut.

Closing my eyes, I soared over distant heights.

Hours later, I came awake with a snap. I lay on a bed of pillows. Through a huge barred window I saw the palace courtyard, where shadowcats in riot gear patrolled.

Prisoner. I groaned. Glass had betrayed me after all, I thought. *But at least we got Hatter.*

I rose, and found the scar-faced shadowcat seated by the door. He snapped to attention. I just stared.

"What's the idea?" I asked.

"Sir?"

I gestured. "All this . . ." And then their proclaiming me the new ruler of Fishtown came flooding back. Eyes wide, I stared at him. "Am I—"

"This way, sir. They're waiting for you."

"Who?"

He opened the door, grinning that scarred grin. Since no answers seemed forthcoming, I decided to play along, at least for the moment. Perhaps a chance to bolt would present itself later. And I *was* leaving first chance.

Scar-face escorted me to a lift, then down we went through security gate after security gate. The shadowcats on duty all snapped to attention and saluted me smartly. I didn't like their smugly self-satisfied looks, not at all. My skin crawled.

Finally we reached the lowest levels, where Hatter must have lived. We got out and, side by side, made our way down long, echoing hallways.

I found myself staring at the decadent opulence around me with growing disgust. Crystal chandeliers, marble floors, stretches of plush red carpet, even busts of Napoleon Bonaparte, Julius Caesar, Patrick Dole, and other great leaders.

When we reached the end of the hall, I heard the pleasant, almost musical tinkle of flowing water from behind a shimmerscreen.

"Go in," scar-face said, and he sat and waited.

I swallowed uneasily, then, with head held high, I walked through.

Colored lights strobed across my eyes, then I found myself in a beautiful garden. Flowers bloomed everywhere, on trellises, in neat little beds, their scent as sweet as anything I'd ever tasted. A fountain bubbled and frothed in the middle of the room, marble cats all around its central basin. Water poured from between stone paws into lesser basins, and that was the sound I'd heard. Many meters overhead arched a pastel blue ceiling, with holographic clouds floating lazily across.

I moved forward, wondering at everything around me. I almost missed the little Japanese pagoda off to the side. But the man seated there cleared his throat, and I whirled to look at him.

It was Glass, of course, dressed in a fancy suit and sipping some fruity drink. He smiled at me, and it was a look of such supreme arrogance, such intolerable superiority, that it stopped me cold.

"What are you doing here?" I demanded.

"Why, I came to congratulate you, of course. And to let you know SecurNet is backing you one hundred percent."

"I don't *want* to rule Fishtown!"

"You can't cut off the head of an organization like this one and not expect it to grow back," he said. "You seemed the perfect choice, so full of milk-and-honey kindness. I would've thought you'd *want* the job."

"Not me," I said quickly. "I don't know anything about running Fishtown. I'm scared to death of shadowcats—"

He laughed. "You'll learn to like them. They're here to protect you, to look after your every need. You'll find soon enough that they're also a very effective bureaucracy. They'll run things. You don't have to do much. Just make occasional public appearances, give speeches when necessary, and press paws with the great and near-great."

"Feh!" I spat. "I'll die here!"

"Eventually."

I stopped. Suddenly Hatter's palace seemed more a cage, or perhaps . . . a prison?

"You'll get used to it," Glass said a moment later. "Power is very addictive, Slash. And don't forget what you told me—you *want* to help catkind. Remember?"

"Yes," I said. "But I didn't mean *me*!"

"They never do." He laughed, almost kindly. "You're a prime example of a survivor-type, Slash, and I know you'll come out on top of things. You always have."

"Thanks," I said slowly. "I think."

"Look," he said, "you *can* back out if you want to. I'll let you. You can go back to raiding dogs, or whatever you want. But it would be a mistake."

"Why?"

"You know what's really going on. Are you going to be happy if you can't do anything about it? If we just pick a shadowcat, shove him into lion skintights, and stick him in power?"

"No," I said. "I guess I don't have any choice, do I?"

"That's the spirit." He rose and nodded to me. "Why don't you take the day to wander through your new home. Just ask anyone anything. They'll help you. That's what they're here for."

"I will."

He patted me on the shoulder as he left. I watched the shimmerscreen crackle around him, and then he was gone.

I had a distant, cold sort of feeling inside, as though all the fight had been sucked out of me. And slowly, so very slowly I made a circuit of the room, looking at all the beautiful flowers, watching them sway in the breeze from the ventilators.

Only when I tried to pick one did I discover they were all plastic. Somehow it figured.

* * *

I met with Glass and dozens of other officials through the next week. Hatter's job seemed more public relations than anything else, keeping alive an image of kindness and generosity and yes, even power. Catkind had to be protected, didn't it? I told myself that. I told myself I'd make a better leader than any of the shadowcats.

Rex called one night. "I want to congratulate you," he said, smiling his collie smile.

I just snarled and tabbed off the vidphone. The war with dogs, my own personal one, still lay too fresh in memory to accept all these changes at once.

But then I immediately regretted cutting him off. Hatter had said we had more in common with dogkind than with humans. And the shadowcats worked alongside Rex's dogs. I knew that; I'd seen the reports.

Finally I dug up Rex's number (I had Hatter's files at my disposal) and dialed him back.

"I want to apologize," I said. "You just caught me off guard."

"No matter." He grinned, tongue hanging out. "We wanted to invite you to dinner next week. If you have time?"

"Sure," I said. "I'd like that." I could hardly refuse now, I thought.

And he really wasn't so bad, I discovered as we talked. He had a wife and five pups, and when he showed me their pictures over the vidphone, I melted inside. Like Paul, he'd become a person rather than just another *dog* to hate.

Later that day, at a meeting with Glass (we were going over rosters of shadowcats—four hundred and thirty-six of them in all, to a cat on SecurNet's payroll), I asked why SecurNet bothered with catkind at all. "Why not just have feet patrol Fishtown, same as the rest of the Sprawl?"

He smiled as though he'd expected the question. "It's

necessary to have private organizations, just as it's necessary to control them from within. They give people with goals and ambitions a place to go . . . an alternative, if you will, to government service.''

"But it *is* government service.''

"They don't find out till they're in." He chuckled. "And sometimes not even then!"

"Why doesn't that make me feel any better?" I asked.

Weeks blurred to months. SecurNet surgeons altered me to lionform, "so you're more imposing." Of course, they didn't give me a chance to object. So I accepted it, and fell into the routine of my new life.

I never saw Hangman or any of my old friends these days. SecurNet kept me too busy, going to official functions, making carefully scripted speeches. Once I even visited Congress and spoke, along with Rex and several other animalform leaders, to a subcommittee. A senator asked me for a report on catkind.

"They"—(Why did I find myself speaking of catkind as "they?")—"don't pose an immediate threat," I said. "They're content and complacent."

The senators nodded knowingly. Several wrote that down as though it meant something.

Eventually I realized there was a degree of self-rule among all the branches of SecurNet: it was too big for any one person to govern with any degree of effectiveness, even someone like Glass. When I'd settled in, become used to the routine, they allowed me more and more responsibility. I arranged for shadowcats to trail those catmen who attracted SecurNet's interest. I allowed mail to be intercepted, private files tapped, order kept among the various organizations in Fishtown through fear of my shadowcats.

Hangman had set up his own dog-raiding business. I left

him strictly alone, and now I realized why Hatter had let me operate. Individuals truly *didn't* matter. Only the whole of catkind did; individuals could do what they wanted, unless they tried to change the status quo, dam the flow of events bearing animalkind along in the channel SecurNet had cut for it. A balancing act, indeed.

But I found I missed my old friends, my old life. One day the urge hit me to see Hangman again, and I told my shadowcats to invite him to the palace.

"You can fit him in just after eleven," they told me. "No more than fifteen minutes, though. You have a meeting."

"Great," I said. Then I remembered Hangman's hatred of shadowcats, his fear of being arrested. "He might not cooperate," I said, "but I don't want any violence. If he won't come, leave him there."

They nodded agreeably. Then I found myself swamped with reading and approving commerce reports, and didn't have time to worry about him.

Some hours later, during a milk break, they ushered Hangman in to see me.

"Welcome, welcome!" I said, rising from a pillow.

He just stared, a look of disgust on his face. Finally he said, "Bastard."

"What's wrong?"

"I don't like shadowcats bursting into my home."

"I'm sorry," I said. "I ordered them to be polite."

He shrugged. "What is it?"

"I just . . . wanted to see you again. We're friends, remember? Do I need a special excuse to say hello?"

"We're not friends," he said. "Not anymore. Not after what you've done."

"What—"

"Look!" he said. "You're no better than Hatter was. You sold out. You're part of SecurNet!"

"I'm needed here—"

"Sure," he sneered. "Think that. Just stay away from me!" Then he turned and stalked out, tail held high, steel claws tapping on the marble floor.

I didn't have time, or I might have cried. A shadowcat came in as soon as he left, appointment book in hand, and began sketching out the rest of the day's agenda.

Time passed, days bleeding into weeks, months into years. One morning I woke and looked in the mirror. I found Hatter's face there, old and leonine, all velvet from soft living. *This isn't me*, I thought. *I'm not like that. I'm working for the good of all catkind*.

But it was Hatter in the mirror, gazing out with deep, sad, soulful eyes. Much as I tried, I couldn't see myself anymore. Even dead I hated Hatter, hated the way he looked.

His image would haunt me the rest of my life.

461

Fantasy Books by Richard Knaak